Enchanted Evening

A Magical Mystery from the Enchanted Antique Shop

Cielle Kenner

Welcome to Enchanted Springs, where ghosts are friendly, magic is real, and time is anything but linear.

This story is a work of fiction. Get maps, character profiles, and free bonus content at ciellekenner.com.

Claim your copy of *Death and Doughnuts*, a free mini mystery from the Enchanted Oven bakery! bit.ly/deathanddoughnuts

ISBN 978-0-9729335-4-4
ASIN B0CVZR2QCP

Contents

CHAPTER 1

Ghosts Love Drama

G HOSTS LOVE DRAMA. THE more energy they can stir up, the more alive they feel.

That might not be the case for every ghost, but it's true for the ones I've met at the Enchanted Antique Shop—like Violet, the 1920s flapper who pops in whenever she's looking for excitement.

Not that she always gets her wish. More often than not, she catches me in the middle of my most mundane tasks.

I was at my desk when she made one of her most recent appearances. That evening, as a storm brewed outside, the shop felt especially timeless. I was checking old invoices against packing slips and receipts, trying to document our ever-expanding inventory. I could feel my auburn curls frizzing in the humid air, matching my frazzled mood.

Beside me, Sadie Arragon, tall and willowy, was examining a lamp. Her platinum hair, cut into a chic French bob with bangs, made her look like she had stepped out of a distant, more glamorous past—appropriate, given her dual life as both a history professor and a spellcaster.

In the front parlor, Eleanor Somerville was crocheting in her favorite rocking chair. She was ostensibly retired, but she still came into the shop almost every day. She was tiny, like a bird, complete with a feather-like nest of silver-white curls piled atop her head.

Twila, the shop's spectral Siamese kitten, was cat napping in Eleanor's yarn basket.

That's when I felt it—an electrical charge that raised the hair on my arms, a telltale sign that Violet was about to make an appearance. The scent of fresh roses wafted through the room, so aromatic I actually sneezed. A needle skipped on the old Victrola, and a raucous jazz tune erupted.

I looked up in time to see a swirl of shooting stars as Violet materializing in the center of the shop. Her laughter, echoing like a melody from a forgotten era, filled the room. The spectral beads and feathers on her dress swayed as she moved, making her look like a silent movie star caught in a loop of her most glamorous moment.

"Hello, my pets!" Violet's greeting echoed through the air. "Tonight I bring you news from the Netherworld!"

I was still getting used to Violet, and the shop, and my new life in my old hometown. Since I had moved back to Enchanted Springs, I'd learned more than I ever dreamed possible about the paranormal world that parallelled our own. Ghosts, spirits, magical beings, and immortals didn't haunt the shadows of existence. They were part and parcel of our reality—especially here in Enchanted Springs.

I should know. I was one of them. And trust me, that fact had surprised me more than anyone.

Violet wasn't just any visitor: she was our most prominent ghost, and she came with her own traveling light show. I watched as she completed her manifstation, mesmerized by the rainbow-colored prisms that flashed and sparkled as her spectral form took shape.

Violet had been dead for over a century, but a little thing like mortality hadn't dampened her love of life. As she floated gently down to earth, she spun gracefully, her laughter light and musical, carrying the timeless joy of the Roaring Twenties into the quiet of our modern setting.

Her eyes, bright and mischievous, scanned the room, landing on each of us with a twinkling sparkle. Twila woke up, sensing the change in the atmosphere, and stretched. Violet bent down to scoop the kitten into her arms, and the cat climbed higher, draping herself over Violet's shoulders like a fashionable stole. Violet twirled around, the cat riding along, wrapped around her like a shimmering scarf.

Violet floated across the room, the hem of her dress gliding over the floor without ever quite touching it. She stopped in her tracks when she saw Sadie and me bogged down in busy work, then shook her head in exasperation.

"I swear, youth is wasted on the young. Look at you, two lovely creatures in the prime of life! Yet here you are, surrounded by dust motes and lost hopes, lost and lonely in an old woman's antique shop."

Eleanor set her crochet hook down in her lap, eyes blazing. "I beg your pardon, Violet."

I braced for impact, worried that Eleanor had taken offense to being called "old." Instead, Eleanor defended her housekeeping.

"This shop is *not* dusty. This shop is immaculate. Even if I'm not the proprietor anymore, we haven't retired our magic cleaning elves."

Violet waved a dismissive gloved hand in her direction. "Figure of speech, Ellie. You were their age once. Is this the life you would choose for these pretty young things?"

Eleanor looked at Sadie and me, considering. "Now that you mention it, no."

Violet swooped over to my desk, waving a finger in my face. "Marley, you simply *can't* spend another evening buried in paperwork! If I were in your Mary Janes, I swear I'd die of boredom."

"I hate to break it to you, Violet, but you're already dead."

"Exactly! That's how dreary your life looks, even from this side of the veil."

She sighed, setting the kitten down on my desk. Twila skittered across the surface, knocking a stack of old bank statements to the floor, then scampered back to her comfortable basket of yarn.

Violet merely shrugged, then continued with her announcement. "Luckily, I know just the thing to release you from this charmless life of servitude. There's a murder mystery dinner at *Spirits* speakeasy this Friday, and you're all invited."

As Violet's declaration lingered in the air, she waved her hands with a flourish. Three elegant envelopes materialized. They glided toward us, each sealed with a daub of red wax.

I reached out, catching one before it hit me in the chin. The paper was thick and slightly textured beneath my fingertips. I watched with wonder as the wax seal spontaneously snapped in two and the envelope opened. The card inside unfurled and hovered in the air before me as if held by an unseen hand.

I glanced over at Eleanor and Sadie; their invitations had also taken wing.

A man's voice, deep and resonant, filled the room, narrating the hand-lettered calligraphy.

"You are cordially invited to an evening of magic and mystery at the celebrated *Spirits* speakeasy. Please join us for a paranormal production of 'The Crimson Heist.'"

The ethereal voice continued, setting the stage for an evening that promised to be anything but ordinary.

"Dress in your finest 1920s evening wear and prepare to step back in time, as *Spirits* opens its doors to a night where fact and fiction merge with the fantastical. Witness a tale of theft and treachery that you won't soon forget. Will you unravel the mystery before the night is over, or will the secrets of 'The Crimson Heist' remain shrouded in the mists of time?"

As the invitation concluded, the card gently settled into my hand, the last word echoing softly in the charged air, leaving a trail of spectral resonance.

"Oh, I'm already planning to be there." Eleanor had picked up her crocheting again, and she was rocking back and forth in time with her stitches. "I'm helping Clara with the desserts."

My grandmother Clara and Eleanor were best friends. Gram owned the Enchanted Oven bakery across the street.

At her announcement, Eleanor's invitation disappeared in a puff of lavender-colored smoke.

Meanwhile, Sadie was slipping her invitation back into the envelope, frowning with disappointment. "I can't go. I'm expecting an old friend from Salem this weekend."

But as she spoke, the address on the envelope shimmered and danced, the ink flowing like liquid shadows. I watched in amazement as the elegant script changed from, "Professor Sarah Prospera Arragon" to "Professor Sarah Prospera Arragon and Professor Benedict Sable Cumberwell."

Sadie looked at Violet, and her jaw dropped in surprise. She shook her head in confusion.

"How did you know his name? Benedict only messaged me today, and I haven't told anyone about his visit."

Violet shrugged. "Wasn't me. You'll have to ask Lucius."

"Who?"

"Lucius Black. I'm only the messenger, kiddo. He's the wizard who owns *Spirits*, and he'll be your host for the evening. Let's just say he has his own way of making magic happen, and his talents extend far beyond simple hospitality."

CHAPTER 2

This Could Work

S ADIE LOOKED DOWN AT her invitation, nodding. "You know, this could actually work. Benedict would love a mystical adventure. He was my professor of paranormal studies at the Salem Center for Magical Research. I'd say dinner at a paranormal speakeasy is right up his alley."

Violet grinned and turned toward me. "What about you, poppet? Are you free this Friday?" She popped her gum before I could answer. "Just kidding. Look at you! You've been free every Friday since we first met."

I sighed. We'd only known each other a few months, and my life had changed enormously in that short time.

Before I met Violet, I was a professional photographer in Miami. I was happy, and busy, when suddenly I started seeing visions of the past. Wherever I looked, people and places from decades ago were superimposed over the present, like old-fashioned double negatives. They didn't go away when I looked through my viewfinder, either. Those living flashbacks, where the veil of time shimmered and thinned, revealed glimpses of history. I could even capture ghosts on film—or on memory cards, as the case may be.

I was confused and more than a little concerned for my mental health. I headed back to Enchanted Springs, my small hometown in Central Florida, and confided everything to my grandmother Clara.

That's when I discovered I was simply going through my Saturn Return, an astrological rite of passage that hits everyone as they approach their thirtieth birthdays. And as luck would have it, I also learned I was the latest in a long line of time-traveling witches.

Grandma Clara and her friend Eleanor became my mentors. When Eleanor retired and I became the new proprietor of the Enchanted Antique Shop, I started weaving my own story into the rich tapestry of this mystical town.

As Violet waited for my response, Eleanor chimed in. "You two are new here, but let me tell you, *Spirits* dinner invitations are hard to come by. You're very lucky to get on the list!"

Violet's form shimmered slightly with excitement as she added to Eleanor's observation. "She's right, you know. You probably made the cut because you've already solved a few mysteries around here. You've got a reputation, kiddos!"

I looked over at Sadie, who smiled at me. "Word gets around. Some of my students have even mentioned our exploits in class. They all want to hear about that murder in the Stevens Mansion."

"Okay. As it happens, I do happen to be free on Friday—but not because I'm a recluse or anything." I looked into Violet's eyes, hoping she wasn't pulling a fast one on us. "Are you sure it's really just a murder mystery dinner?" I knew from experience that the paranormal community had a way of living life to the extreme.

Violet did a little dance, swiveling her hips and pumping her fist like she'd won a bet. "Yes! I promise you, kitten. It's all for fun—and it's exactly the sort of adventure you need to break the bleak monotony of nights like this." She curled her lip in disgust as she surveyed my desktop again.

Violet leaned forward, her spectral form casting an ethereal glow in the dim light of the shop. "Let me give you a taste of what you'll experience. First, you can expect one of the most elaborate dinners of your life. Not only dinner, but drinks, and dancing, and desserts from the best baker in town." She turned to wink at Eleanor; she was referring, of course, to my grandmother. "The mystery is scripted, and all of the parts will be played by *Spirits* regulars—our very own cast of paranormal players."

Her voice lowered to a dramatic whisper.

"The mystery itself is steeped in secrets and hidden motives. You'll be part of the audience, but in a setting like this, everyone is part of the story. And given your skills at solving mysteries, you'll probably figure it out before anyone else."

Sadie, now clutching her invitation, looked puzzled. "But the Lydia Hotel? How can any party happen there? It's been abandoned for ages. It's practically falling in on itself."

Eleanor smiled. "That's all part of the illusion. Enchanted Springs' most fabulous speakeasy is hidden in plain sight... if you're lucky enough to have the sight, that is."

Violet's gaze shifted to me, a playful smirk forming on her lips as she noticed my hesitation. "Well, if Sadie is bringing her friend Benedict, that leaves Marley as a third wheel." She opened her eyes wide as if she was simply asking an innocent question, but her voice lilted with a hint of mischief. "Why don't you invite Jack to be your escort?"

I hesitated. The thought of inviting Jack Edgewood—the enigmatic vampire detective—sent an unfamiliar flutter through my chest. Yes, we had worked together to solve a few mysteries, but the idea of a date with him made me feel more nervous than excited.

"I don't know, Violet," I began, trying to brush off the suggestion. "Jack and I aren't exactly friends. I don't think he thinks of me that way. Whenever we've been together in the past, he's always been strictly professional."

From her rocking chair, Eleanor looked up, the twinkle in her eyes belying her age. "Oh, honey, we've seen the way he looks at you. It's anything but *professional*." As she teased gently, a knowing smile spread across her face.

Sadie nodded in agreement, her face also brightening with amusement. "Seriously, Marley. How could you not have noticed? Every time he comes into the shop or you bump into each other at the bakery, he doesn't have eyes for anyone but you."

Flustered by their observations, I felt my cheeks warm. Jack was undeniably attractive. He had old-world charm and an aura of mystery that seemed to cling to him like a shadow.

"Besides," Sadie added with a grin, "it's not every day you get to go to a speakeasy murder mystery dinner with a vampire detective. Think of the fun you'll have!"

"Perfect!" Violet exclaimed. "It's settled then. A night of enchantment and a little bit of danger—but the fun kind, of course."

Her smile broadened, her gaze shifting playfully to me. It wasn't settled yet, but I was considering the possibility.

"And Marley, do tell Jack to turn in his detective badge for the evening. This is a party, not a police procedural." She followed her quip with a light laugh.

Her comment eased some of my apprehension, reminding me that the night was meant for fun and mystery, not the usual grit and seriousness of our usual encounters. "I dunno. It's not like I can ask him to leave his detective instincts at the door."

"Well, if the two of you figure it out early, sit on it for a bit and leave a little fun for the rest of us."

Violet's laughter echoed softly around the shop, and I found myself considering the idea more seriously. Jack was indeed a man in mystique. He'd once confided that he was over a century old, his life extended and transformed by his vampiric nature. Despite his eternal youth, he carried a wisdom and a weariness that only those who have lived through many eras possess. His insights into the supernatural had proved invaluable in our past adventures, and his presence could certainly make an intriguing evening even more so.

Taking a deep breath, I finally conceded, the prospect suddenly seeming not only inevitable, but appealing. "All right, I'll ask him. It could be... interesting."

I was ready to shift the attention away from my relationship with Jack. "What about you, Violet? Will you be on the arm of anyone special?"

Her laughter faded into a softer, sadder smile. "I'm a married woman, doll. Death might have parted us, but..." Her voice trailed off, and a distant look clouded her eyes.

I suddenly realized that for all her interactions with us, Violet had revealed very little of her own story. "How long has it been since you've seen each other?"

Violet's expression turned unexpectedly serious, her usual vibrancy dimming.

"That's the thing. I haven't seen him, not since... well, not since it happened. I keep hoping he'll turn up one of these days." The longing in her voice was palpable. It was a stark contrast from her usual ebullience.

Eleanor noticed the shift in Violet's mood.

"Let's not dwell on the shadows of the past tonight." She rose to her feet with a gentle smile. "Violet, we have a new collection of records that you probably haven't heard in a while. How about we put one on?"

As she spoke, Eleanor walked over to the old Victrola. She rifled through the newly arrived collection of records and pulled one out with a flourish. "Ah, here's one you'll like. Bix Beiderbecke, *Singin' the Blues*."

Violet's demeanor brightened instantly. "Are you kidding me? That's one of my favorites!"

Eleanor placed the record on the turntable and wound it up. Soon, the soulful strains of Bix Beiderbecke's cornet filled the shop, the upbeat tempos and brassy solos sweeping away any melancholy that lingered in the air.

Violet sighed with pleasure. "Oh, this takes me back." She clapped her hands, turning toward Sadie and me. "Now, let's get those feet moving! The Charleston isn't going to dance itself. You'll need to learn a few steps if you're going to survive a night at *Spirits*."

With the music setting a playful backdrop, Violet started showing us some basic dance steps, her form flickering rhythmically to the beat. Sadie and I followed along, laughing as we tried to mimic her moves. The dance was infectious, and soon, even Eleanor was caught up in the fun, all of us kicking our heels.

The shop, filled with music and movement, felt like a portal to another time. For a moment, we were all transported to the Roaring Twenties, with its carefree spirit and boundless energy.

"See, doll? There's nothing like a good dance to make life worth living again."

Violet was right. When I followed her lead, everything seemed brighter—at least for a few days.

Until I found myself standing with a magical necklace vibrating at my throat and a dead body at my feet.

———⚹———

In hindsight, maybe I should have known better. Magic always has a price. And when the bill came due at *Spirits*, I knew we would have to pay.

The night had started with such promise—glittering dresses, sparkling glasses, and an air of enchantment that made everything feel surreal. Yet, beneath the glamour and charm, a sinister undercurrent flowed, one that I couldn't quite place until it was too late.

As I stood there, the weight of the scene crashing down on me, part of me wished I could have traveled back in time to decline that invitation. Instead, my gaze locked onto the lifeless eyes of a man sprawled at my feet. His white dinner jacket was now marred by a dark, spreading stain. The ghostly flicker of candlelight cast macabre shadows across his features, and the room seemed to hold its breath.

The performance had gone off script, and it was my responsibility to rewrite the ending.

I felt Jack's presence beside me, his usually steady demeanor shaken by the unexpected turn of events. His voice, usually so composed, wavered as he spoke. "Marley, we need to find out who did this—and why."

The promise of a night of enchantment had twisted into a perilous game of deceit and danger. And as I stared at the body, I knew that uncovering the truth would mean delving into the deepest secrets of the supernatural world—before anyone else became a victim.

CHAPTER 3

Mystery Date

THE MORNING AFTER THE surprise invitation from *Spirits*, I stopped into my grandmother's bakery, the Enchanted Oven. The comforting aroma of freshly baked doughnuts and coffee wrapped around me like a warm blanket. I was here for my usual caffeine fix, but today, I had another mission, too. If I didn't ask Jack to accompany to the dinner, I would never hear the end of it.

I spotted Jack sitting at one of the small tables by the window, a newspaper spread out in front of him. He looked every bit the modern detective, with his sharp jawline and deep-set eyes that seemed to hold centuries of secrets. He wore a tailored grey jacket that hinted at a bygone era, his tie knotted just so, and his dress shoes polished to an impossibly black shine.

He glanced up as I approached him, and the morning light caught the hint of gold in his blue eyes. I couldn't tell if they were reflecting the sun or glowing with an inner light. Once again, I was impressed by his ability to withstand sunlight. The effect was both captivating and slightly unnerving.

His expression shifted subtly from contemplation to a guarded welcome, and he gestured for me to take a seat. There was always a certain intensity about him, a seriousness that came with his role as a policeman—and as a preternatural guardian. Yet, in moments like these, caught in the mundane act of reading the newspaper over coffee, Jack almost seemed ... human.

"Morning, Jack." I tried to sound casual as I slid the invitation across the table toward him. "Look what I got."

He studied the hand-written calligraphy with a critical eye, then looked back at me. "Looks pretty swanky."

"Well, I've never been there, but Eleanor suggested I ask you to be my plus one."

As he looked back at me, his expression softened. "Would I be attending in my professional capacity? Does Eleanor think you need a bodyguard?"

I laughed. "No. Both Eleanor and Violet have assured me it's all good, clean fun."

He arched an eyebrow. "Maybe. But if it's happening at *Spirits*, I can tell you that those paranormal parties hardly ever go to plan." He was trying to sound official, but the slight curve of his lips suggested that he wasn't entirely serious.

I couldn't help but be drawn in by the rare smile. I appreciated once again how his presence seemed to straddle the line between the mysterious and the familiar. Jack was a puzzle, a creature of the night who navigated the modern world with an ease that belied his true nature. He was powerful enough to endure sunlight, but still human enough to care about truth and justice. Yet sitting here with him, discussing plans as ordinary as attending a dinner party, he was just Jack—less the undead detective and more the charming companion. Who knows? If he kept it up, he could even be the life of the party.

I leaned forward, resting my chin on my hand, a playful glint in my eye. "Wouldn't it be fun to solve a make-believe mystery for a change?" I was teasing, imagining us embroiled in a theatrical caper rather than the real dangers we'd faced together in the past. "You know, where the biggest risk is overacting, not actual danger."

Before he could respond, Gram came over with a fresh pot of coffee and spotted the invitation on the table. "Oh, the *Spirits* soiree! I'm so glad you'll both be there." She beamed as she poured a refill for Jack, then poured a fresh cup for me. "Clara and I will be helping Sylvia Robinson with the main courses, and I'm planning to whip up some extra special desserts."

Jack's eyes lit up. "You don't say!" It was no secret that Sylvia was the best chef in Enchanted Springs, just like my grandmother was the best baker. Jack and I had first met at a party that Sylvia catered, and despite the little bit of murder that put a damper on the festivities, we both had fond memories of her buffet.

He smiled, and for a moment, he looked like a kid in a candy shop. "If Sylvia is cooking, I'd be a fool to say no."

Jack's gaze drifted to the window as if picturing the evening ahead. After a moment, he turned back to me, a decisive nod forming. "All right, you've convinced me. A night of gourmet dining is too good to pass up. And who knows? Maybe it'll be a quiet evening without any... unnecessary excitement."

With a chuckle and a sense of relief, I clinked my coffee cup against his. "To a night of good food and good company, then," I toasted, pleased that Sylvia's culinary reputation had tipped the scales in my favor.

The morning air was crisp as I left the bakery, a cup of coffee to go in one hand and a bag of doughnuts in the other. I was ready to open the Enchanted Antique Shop for the day. The quiet of the early hours was one of my favorite times in Enchanted Springs, peaceful and unassuming.

As I crossed the street to the shop, a sudden gust of wind swept down the avenue. As the wind howled, papers from nearby trash bins swirled in the air, its chill biting through the calm. It was unusual for Florida—even for Enchanted Springs—and it sent a shiver down my spine. Quickening my pace, I was eager to step into the familiar warmth of the shop.

No sooner had I unlocked the front door and stepped inside than the ground beneath my feet gave a peculiar shudder. It felt as if something deep beneath the earth was stirring, awakening. Then, as quickly as it had begun, it stopped. The wind died down, and an eerie silence followed.

What was going on?

I stood stock still, waiting to see if anything else would happen. I couldn't hear anything but silence.

I was about to dismiss it all as a trick of my imagination when the antique chandelier in the entryway began to sway gently. Then I heard a rustling in the corner, near Eleanor's chair.

My first thought was Twila, the spectral Siamese kitten. There were times when she scampered through the shop, and while she was normally a graceful little cat, she was still a kitten—a perpetual kitten—and there were times when her oversized paws got ahead of her and she knocked curios and figurines to the floor.

Something was moving, but it wasn't Twila. I looked around, and over near Eleanor's chair, Twila was standing on full alert, watching, entranced, at something I couldn't see.

I followed her gaze to the old Victrola. As I watched, one of the old records from our new collection floated up into the air. The disc emerged from the paper sleeve and settled gently on the player.

"Violet, is that you?"

There was no response. I didn't really expect one—at least not from Violet. She never walked in like a normal person. When Violet made an appearance, she ensured that all eyes were on her, with lights, sound, and a celestial accompaniment to trumpet her entrance.

Of course, that didn't mean this wasn't merely the first step in her next materialization. I called again. "Violet?" But no. She wasn't there.

I took a deep breath and focused my intuition, the way Grandma Clara and Eleanor had been teaching me. I could definitely sense another presence in the room, but it felt as though it was coming from a distance, from long ago and far away. If I had to guess, the visiting spirit was using all of its energy simply to move the needle into place.

Sure enough, as the music began to play, the ghostly energy dissipated completely.

The song, however, was mesmerizing.

The ruby sun sets,
The day fades away.
I have no regrets.
My love is here to stay.

The sound was haunting—a woman's voice, lilting and clear despite the static and pops of the old record. I paused, listening, drawn to the sadness in the song. It was a voice crying out from another time, filled with a poignant longing.

"Hello?" I called out, half expecting someone to answer. No response came, only the continuation of that melancholic tune.

As the song reached its end, I reached out and lifted the needle. The shop fell eerily quiet. As I glanced down, my eyes caught sight of the record label, worn and faded but legible enough. I didn't recognize the singer's name, but the song title struck a chord: The Ruby Sun.

I carefully placed the record back in its sleeve as Sadie breezed in, her teaching materials in hand, ready for her day at Magnolia University. "Hey, Marley. I left one some of my lecture plans here in all the excitement last night."

Noticing my distracted gaze lingering on the record player, she arched an eyebrow. "What's going on?"

"It's that record. It just floated up and started playing itself."

She moved over to the Victrola, where I'd left the record leaning against the cabinet.

"Is this the one?" She studied it carefully. "It looks like all the others. Why do you suppose it was playing?"

"Well, I thought it might be Violet, but obviously, she's not here."

She set her purse down long enough to pull out her phone and snap a photo of the record label. "If I have any free time today, I'll do a little research. I might even stop by the music department to see if any of the professors there know anything about the singer or the production company."

I watched her with a mixture of awe and gratitude. Sadie had a way of diving into mysteries with the same fervor she approached her historical studies. I knew the type: both of my parents were professors. Sadie had actually come to Enchanted Springs to fill in for my mother, who was off with my stepfather on an extended archaeological dig in Central America. In Sadie's short time at the school, she had become an integral part of the university and the community.

Most people didn't know that Sadie was a historian by day, and a spellcaster by night. I'd met her during the Founders Festival, when I first discovered my own magical heritage.

Now, as she focused on the mysteriously self-playing record, her face lit up with the thrill of the chase. It was moments like these—watching her piece together the puzzles of the past—that reminded me how lucky I was to have her by my side.

"Thanks, Sadie." The odd turn of events had me feeling flustered, but I was impressed by her no-nonsense approach. "I don't know what I'd do without you."

She flashed a quick grin. "Probably get buried under a mountain of enchanted artifacts. Now, I've got to dash. History waits for no man—or rather, my history students wait for no woman. If I'm not there when they get to class, they think they've won a free day off."

With a playful salute, she grabbed her bag and headed for the door.

CHAPTER 4

An Era of Elegance

I SPENT THE REST of the day deep in thought, the haunting tune from the old record player looping endlessly in my mind. For a song that probably hadn't been heard in over a century, it clung to my thoughts with surprising tenacity.

The shop was unusually quiet that day, a rare respite that allowed me to drift through my chores almost mechanically. I finished clearing my desk, then busied myself with dusting the china figurines and sweeping the old wood floors. Every stroke of the broom helped sweep the eerie melody into the background.

Twila had vanished shortly after Sadie's departure. Her absence was as mysterious as her comings and goings. Eleanor made a brief appearance, her visit fleeting as she excused herself for a Garden Club luncheon. "They're expecting a full house today." With a wave, she was gone, likely swept up in the bustle of her afternoon, leaving the shop in silence once more.

As the hours ticked by, the slow tick of the clock and the quiet made the shop feel more like a time capsule, sealed away from the modern hustle. When I finally flipped the "open" sign to "closed" for the day, the soft click of the lock echoed unusually loud in the empty space.

I lingered in the quiet aftermath, waiting for Sadie. Together, we were set on a mission: to comb through the shop's treasure trove of vintage clothing, in search of gowns that would transport us from the twenty-first century to the Roaring Twenties.

She arrived like a whirlwind, bursting through the door with irrepressible zeal. Her energy was infectious, and I found myself swept up in her enthusiasm.

We moved to the back of the shop, where dresses from decades past hung on hangers, many in zippered bags. We admired the colors and fabrics from bygone eras.

"Look at this one, Marley!" Sadie exclaimed, holding up a knee-length polka-dot dress that screamed 1950s. Its red fabric popped against the more subdued tones of the surrounding garments.

I chuckled, plucking a sleek, navy blue sheath dress from a nearby rack. "And this could be straight out of a 60s spy movie. Can you imagine sneaking around in this, martini in hand?"

Sadie's laughter mingled with mine. "Only if I can wear this," she said, waving a mustard yellow dress with a smart collar and a cheeky hem above the knee. "It's got that perfect blend of secretary and *seductress*."

We finally decided to get serious. Several dresses from the 1920s were draped elegantly on padded hangers, each piece a relic of rebellious glamour. They were in amazing condition for their age, and I suspected that Eleanor had worked some magic to keep them from fading or falling prey to moths.

"Look at this one," I said, running my fingers over a dress that shimmered with sequins. The fabric was surprisingly soft. I held it up in front of me. "But wait a minute. It's cut like a flour sack."

Sadie glanced over and laughed. "That's because flappers were trying to liberate themselves from corsets and curvy silhouettes. They wanted their clothing to be comfortable and loose. If you're looking for form-fitting fashion, you're in the wrong decade."

She found a beaded dress that looked promising until she pulled it off the rack. "Ugh. This looks like a tank top with fringe."

I chuckled at Sadie's candid description as she held the dress out for closer examination. The beadwork twinkled under the shop's lights, each strand catching the light with a hint of defiance.

"Maybe so, but think how that fringe would move on the dance floor."

She put it back on the rack. "I'll pass."

Her fingers danced along the clothes rack, the hangers clicking in a rhythmic succession as she slid each dress aside, considering her options. She paused occasionally to fluff a skirt or adjust a strap, her eyes scanning the fabrics and patterns with a discerning gaze. Every so often, she'd pull a dress slightly off the rack, tilting her head as she envisioned how it would look not only on a hanger, but in the full swing of the party.

Sadie's search paused as she drew out a dress that made us both catch our breaths. It was a masterpiece of the 1920s fashion—a cocktail gown crafted from red satin.

"Marley, this is it," Sadie declared, her voice tinged with awe. The fabric shimmered under the shop's lights, the color perfect against her platinum blonde hair. She held it against herself, her face lighting up with a smile. "What do you think?"

She held the dress up to admire it, and as she swung it gently from side to side, it was as if we were transported back in time. I could picture the shop around us morphing into a lavish jazz club, filled with the sounds of a piano and the soft clinking of cocktail glasses.

Without a moment's hesitation, she stripped down to her sports bra and boxer briefs and slipped the dress over her head. It draped gracefully around her figure, falling in soft, fluid lines that suggested motion even in stillness. The dress was gathered at one hip—a stylish detail that also kept the long, V-shaped neckline from falling open.

Sadie raced to a full-length mirror to take it all in. "Can you imagine how daring this must have looked, back in the day?"

As she spoke, I could see her eyes light up with a historian's passion. She wasn't only putting on a dress; she was stepping into the style of the woman who had worn that dress a century ago, who had danced to the jazz rhythms and embraced a new world of possibilities.

"I think it looks daring by today's standards. That V-neck goes all the way down to your bellybutton."

She grinned at me. "I know! It's almost indecent! But when would I ever get another chance to wear something like this in real life?"

Sadie's reflection beamed back at us, a vision of 1920s charm and audacity. "I say we go all out. If we're going to do this, we might as well make it spectacular, right?" She twirled, the satin rippling as she moved, catching the light with every spin.

"Absolutely," I agreed, searching the racks for my own piece of the past to wear. As I shuffled through the hangers, the soft fabrics, embroidered and embellished with sequins, whispered of decades gone by. Finally, my fingers closed around a deep emerald dress that shimmered with promise. The rich color looked like it would complement my auburn hair. "This could work," I said, more to myself than to Sadie.

Pulling it off the rack, I held it against myself, looking to Sadie for approval. "What do you think? Could I pull this off?"

Sadie nodded enthusiastically. "It looks like it was made for you, Marley. That color, the sheen—it's as if the dress was waiting just for you."

I tried it on. Admittedly, the gown was simpler than hers: a graceful scoop neckline dipped below my collarbone. The bodice led seamlessly into a gently flowing skirt that reached below my knees. But as I spun around, craning my neck to see what it looked like from behind, I was sold. On this gown, the back dipped lower than the front, landing between my shoulder blades. The design was both daring and dramatic. While I wouldn't chop my long hair into a daring flapper bob, I could make the most of the style by pulling my curls into a chic, curly updo.

Sadie nodded enthusiastically. "It's perfect. You'll turn heads, guaranteed."

Side by side, Sadie and admired our reflections, the dresses transforming us into echoes of a bold, bygone era. We turned to each other and laughed. "We've found our dresses, Sadie. Let's show them what a couple of modern girls can do with a little vintage flair."

Just as we were complimenting each other's outfits, the air in the corner of the room shimmered, and with a glimmer of iridescent lights and sparkles, Violet materialized. She took in what we were wearing and shook her head emphatically.

"Oh, no, dolls. We're not going to a tea party with little-girl frocks. This is a soiree. You'll need full-length evening gowns."

Sadie and I exchanged a look. I was a little disappointed that we hadn't measured up, but Sadie shrugged nonchalantly and waved her hand in the air, her fingers tracing a graceful arc.

> *Threads of time, once short and sweet,*
> *Stretch your weave down to our feet.*
> *Drape our gowns to touch the floor,*
> *Lengthen them for evermore.*

As her hand moved, magic sparkled around us, and I felt the fabric of my dress ripple and flow downward.

In moments, the transformation was complete. The dresses had elongated into elegant, floor-length gowns that cascaded to the floor in a flow of sumptuous silk. Sadie's red gown featured a tasteful slit up one side, revealing a glimpse of her gracefully arched leg with every step she took. My emerald dress now sported a sweeping train.

"Better." Violet approved with a nod, her own attire flickering as if woven from moonlight and shadows. "Now you're ready for a night to remember."

Sadie twirled, the hem of her gown swirling around her. "Thanks to a little magical alteration—off the cuff, as it were. That wasn't the most lyrical spell I've ever cast, but it did the job."

I looked down at my own gown, the fabric shimmering in the light, and couldn't help but feel a surge of excitement. With our transformed dresses, we were ready to step into the night's mysteries with confidence and style.

CHAPTER 5

Glam and Glitter

"Now for some jewelry. This event calls for a touch of sparkle, don't you think?"

"I'll leave you to it," Violet said. "I've got a few last-minute details to look after myself."

Sadie made a beeline to a display cabinet brimming with vintage costume jewelry. Her eyes lit up when she spotted an art-deco pendant adorned with light green chalcedony and yellow bakelite. "This is stunning," she declared.

She carefully lifted the necklace, admiring the diamond-cut garnet at its center. The gemstone caught the light and sparkled with every subtle movement. Below the pendant, a long tassel of fine gold chains swayed gracefully.

She slipped the necklace over her head. Her smile widened as it fell perfectly into place, complementing the long V-shaped neckline of her dress.

"Good choice," I said. "I think I saw some earrings in the storage room that would be a perfect match." Without waiting for a reply, I darted off toward the back.

The storage room was dimly lit, and the shelves were crowded with hidden treasures waiting to be rediscovered. I found the earrings, but as I reached for them, my sleeve snagged a stack of wicker baskets.

"Oops," I muttered under my breath, quickly scooping them off the floor. Then I noticed a leather box, tucked behind an old globe that had been shifted slightly out of place.

I reached for the box, curious. It was odd; I'd been in this storeroom a hundred times and never noticed it before. With a flick of my fingers, I opened the hinged lid and gasped. Inside, nestled against a faded silk lining, was a pearl necklace with an enormous, ruby-red teardrop pendulum. It was far too large to be real. Between the pearls, crimson gemstones sparkled, accented with clear crystal rondelles.

Holding both treasures, I hurried back to Sadie. "I found the earrings," I said, handing them to her. "But look at this."

Sadie leaned forward and whistled. "Did you pull that out of the safe?"

"Not even. It was just sitting on the shelf, behind the old globe. From the dust on the box, I'd say it's been in there for a while."

I carefully lifted the necklace out. The pearls were cold to the touch, and heavier than I expected.

I decided to wear it, draping it around my neck and fumbling slightly with the hook at the back. I called Sadie over to help with the clasp as I held my hair up. As she fastened it, her fingers paused.

"Oh, that's odd." She laughed softly. "It practically closed on its own. The clasp just slipped into place."

I looked in the mirror, adjusting the oversized ruby pendant so it lay right. The facets of the colored stones captured the light, refracting it into dazzling prisms. Sadie nodded approvingly. "It's perfect, Marley. The red compliments your green dress, and those pearls glow against your skin. It looks like it was made for you."

I stepped back to the mirror to take in the full effect. She was right. The satin fabric of my dress shimmered with each movement, and the gemstones around my neck gleamed. The full effect was completely, totally, one hundred percent elegance.

"We look amazing," Sadie beamed.

As we continued to perfect our outfits, Sadie reached for a pair of satin pumps. They initially shimmered a soft silver under the shop's antique lighting, but with a casual flick of her wrist and a quiet incantation, the pumps transformed, taking on the rich red hue of her dress. "Much better," she declared with satisfaction, her shoes now perfectly coordinated with her gown.

Meanwhile, I spotted a pair of slingback heels crafted of soft ivory leather. Their classic and refined style caught my eye immediately, and I felt no need for any magical adjustments. Slipping them on, I admired how the neutral color contrasted beautifully against the deep emerald of my dress. The heels weren't only a fit for my feet but a fit for the moment.

I leaned closer to adjust a stray curl when it happened. The mirror's surface shimmered, and for a fleeting moment, it wasn't my own reflection staring back at me. There, superimposed over my image, was the figure of a woman dressed in an opulent 1920s evening gown, her attire as authentic and detailed as if she had walked off a movie set. The gown was a masterpiece of the era, adorned with intricate lace and delicate sequins that cascaded down her silhouette.

Most striking were the long, elegant gloves she wore, which matched the creamy hue of her dress, hugging her arms with a grace that spoke of lost times and forgotten dances. Her strawberry blonde hair was curled into ringlets, framing a face that was both haunting and haunted, her eyes meeting mine with an intensity that rooted me to the spot.

As quickly as she appeared, the vision dissolved, leaving me staring at my own reflection, the echo of her presence lingering like perfume in the air. I reached up, my fingers brushing the necklace as I shook off the eerie feeling.

Sadie hadn't seemed to notice, and I didn't want to make a big deal out of yet another ghost in the shop.

"We're ready," I finally said, turning to Sadie with a determined smile. "Whatever Friday night holds in store, we'll handle it in style."

CHAPTER 6

Puttin' on the Ritz

F RIDAY NIGHT HAD ARRIVED, and the Enchanted Antique Shop was again the scene of our transformation. We closed the shop early, so Sadie and I could slip into our vintage dresses. Our excitement was palpable. This wasn't just any night out—it was a chance to experience living history, without the bother of time travel.

As I adjusted the clasp on my necklace, I caught Sadie's eye in the mirror. "It's nice to do this the easy way for once," I mused. Sadie chuckled in agreement, smoothing the front of her dress.

"Definitely easier on the stomach," she said with a wry smile. "No matter how many times we do it, time traveling always leaves me feeling seasick."

I nodded, remembering the swirling sensation and the slight disorientation that accompanied each journey through time. "It's a thrill to see the past first-hand, but there's something to be said for keeping our feet firmly in the present."

Sadie applied a final touch of lipstick and grinned. "Well, tonight we get all the glamour and none of the queasiness. Let's make the most of it."

Aside from the day-to-day management of the store, the most crucial part of my role at the Enchanted Antique Shop was safeguarding a time-travel portal in the storage room. Our building was the oldest structure in town. It was literally a landmark. It had also been built around a magical gateway through time; that was a closely guarded secret. Eleanor and Clara had carefully trained me in the mechanics and the ethics of its use.

Theoretically, the portal could take travelers to any time and place. For the most part, we used it to travel to earlier iterations of the shop, which served as our home base and safe haven during temporal excursions. I'd already used it to double-check some facts in a few investigations. I'd also darted in and out for practical purposes, like retrieving some missing place settings for a Thanksgiving display at the shop.

As we added the final touches to our looks, Sadie's laughter filled the room. She grabbed her phone and waved me over with a mischievous grin. "Come on, Marley, let's capture the moment. It's not every day we get dolled up like this!"

I sidled up next to her, the dress like silk against my skin... which made sense, since it was silk. I simply wasn't used to wearing such fine fabric. The weight of the pearls felt cool around my neck, and the ruby-red pendant nestled at my throat. "Violet, get in here," I called, knowing full well she'd never miss a chance to be in the spotlight.

With a delighted squeal that only a century-old ghost could muster, Violet materialized beside us. She wore a gossamer evening gown that hugged her curves and fell in delicate, flowing layers. Her hair was styled in perfect Marcel waves, topped with a jeweled band around her head. She twirled, a few hand-stitched sequins catching the light with a dazzling effect. "Do you like it?" she beamed, stopping to pose beside me. "It's an authentic design from 1923."

"Violet, you look like you've stepped straight out the Great Gatsby."

Her headband, adorned with beads and a large ornamental jewel, sat perfectly atop her chestnut bob, complementing the embroidery around her neck. "I like how everything you're wearing matches from head to toe."

She gave a pleased, ghostly giggle and fluffed her hair. "Well, it's French. Plus it's all about the ensemble, you know. We took our fashion seriously."

Her spectral form shimmered slightly, a ghostly echo of her flamboyant past, as she struck a pose. Sadie held her phone out, expertly framing us all on the screen, and snapped a couple of playful selfies.

CHAPTER 7

Date Night

A KNOCK AT THE door ended our ersatz photo session. Sadie rushed to open it, allowing a cool evening breeze to sweep into the shop. Her face lit up with recognition and delight, "Benedict! You made it!" She stepped forward to greet him with a warm embrace, which he returned with a gentle pat on her back.

I don't know what I expected, but the sixty-something man she welcomed through the door was a complete surprise. He wasn't much taller than me, which meant Sadie towered over him by a good six inches. What he lacked in height, he made up for in stockiness. The top of his circle-shaped head was as bald as a cue ball, and his round face was accented with a white goatee and a matching mustache. He wore a shiny monocle over his left eye.

He paused inside the doorway, taking in the room with an analytical gaze. His posture was one of refined elegance, underscored by the classic tweed suit and the slightly rumpled shirt he wore. A quirky bow tie added a touch of scholarly flair, along with the bamboo cane hooked over one elbow. He carried a gray felt fedora, which he removed as he entered, holding it against his chest in a gesture of old-world courtesy.

Sadie was practically bouncing up and down with delight. "I'm so glad you could come!"

"Wouldn't miss it for the world. Not only does a 1920s gala sound like a fascinating experience, it also gives me a chance to wear some of the clothes I've had hanging in the back of my closet for longer than I like to admit."

Sadie turned toward me, a bright smile on her face. "Marley, this is Professor Benedict Cumberwell, my former instructor and fellow enthusiast of all things magical and historical. He always had a way of making the complex theories of metaphysics accessible and, more importantly, relevant." She turned to smile at him. "I owe a lot of my understanding of the magical realms to his teachings. And Benedict, this is Marley Montgomery, the heart and soul of the Enchanted Antique Shop."

"Pleasure to meet you, Marley," Benedict said, extending his hand. His grip was firm. "You look stunning, my dear." His voice paused slightly as he spotted my necklace. He squinted a bit, his expression shifting to one of curious scrutiny. "That's an... interesting piece you're wearing."

I touched the pendant, somewhat self-conscious under his intense gaze. "It is pretty, isn't it? I found it here at the shop. I thought it fit the theme tonight."

"Indeed." Benedict's smile thinned slightly, his eyes lingering on the necklace, his mind seeming to drift off into a sort of reverie. "It reminds me of old legends I've read, of voices trapped in silver, of timeless songs woven into the very fabric of this town. Fascinating stuff. I believe a collector of tales could spend a lifetime studying some of the enchanted artifacts in this shop."

His smile returned, and he shrugged a little, as if he was trying to lighten the mood. "I suppose my academic instincts are never fully off."

I chuckled, a bit uneasily. "Well, I hope our little town lives up to your expectations."

"Oh, I suspect it will," he murmured, his gaze briefly traveling back around the room.

"And this is Violet," Sadie continued, gesturing to Violet's spectral form shimmering near the grandfather clock. "She's as much a part of this place as any of the antiques."

Benedict's eyes widened slightly in genuine fascination. "A pleasure, indeed," he said, bowing slightly. Violet curtsied playfully in response. "Charmed, I'm sure."

"It's not often I have the chance to meet a young woman of your—well, your particular persuasion." He cleared his throat. "Perhaps later, I could bend your ear a bit. I'd love to ask you about some of the things I've read. It seems Enchanted Springs is quite a treasure trove. Your opinions could be quite valuable. You could help me separate fact from fiction, as it were."

Behind him, the door swung open again and Jack appeared. "I hope I'm not late."

"You're right on time," I said, urging him forward to join our little group.

I took a moment to admire his attire. He wasn't the modern-day detective we were used to seeing around town, dressed in a button-down shirt and khakis. This version of Jack Edgewood was a debonair figure who seemed to have stepped straight out of the Roaring Twenties. He wore a vintage tuxedo that accentuated his broad shoulders and lean frame. My eyes traced the lines of the fine wool coat that draped across his shoulders, its midnight hue swallowing the dim light around him. His collar, starched to a crisp perfection, framed his jawline with an almost austere precision. A black bow tie nestled neatly at his throat, and the gold cufflinks at his wrists caught the light of the setting sun. Jack's dark blond hair, normally rumpled, was slicked back. He looked suave and sophisticated, like a dashing gentleman who could easily blend into any upscale gathering of the 1920s. He could have rubbed elbows with John D. Rockefeller or Henry Ford. It was a side of Jack I had never seen, and I wasn't just impressed. I was captivated.

"Wow, Jack, you clean up pretty well," I teased.

He responded with a light, self-deprecating laugh, a rare sound. "One does what one can to fit in with such distinguished company." His eyes met mine with a glint of amusement.

Jack stepped further into the shop, pausing to take in the sight before him. His gaze first landed on Violet, and a smile tugged at the corners of his lips. "Miss Serrano, that dress is magnificent. It's like you stepped right out of a Parisian salon."

Turning to Sadie, his smile widened. "And Sadie, you look spectacular. Your beauty would shine in any era, but that gown brings out your inner radiance."

Finally, his eyes found me, and there was a noticeable shift in his expression. A soft, almost imperceptible intensity replaced his casual demeanor as he studied me from head to toe. "Marley," he began, his voice lowering to a tone that was both warm and filled with a hint of awe. "You look... breathtaking." He paused, and as he stepped closer, the dim light caught a brief, unusual glint off his teeth—was it a trick of the light, or something more? "Truly, you are the vision of the evening."

I felt a flutter of unexpected nerves. Jack's usual reserve was replaced by openness, and his look held a depth that suggested tonight was more than a friendly get-together. As he continued to admire my dress, the mystery deepened. I started to wonder about the man behind the detective—and the hint of something else in his smile.

I was speechless. Luckily, I didn't have to say anything. Benedict stepped forward, straightening his shoulders and greeting Jack with a businesslike nod.

"You must be Detective Edgewood. I've heard quite a bit about you. Interesting to finally put a face to the stories."

Jack nodded, his smile polite but guarded. "Professor Cumberwell, I presume? Sadie speaks highly of you." There was a measured tone in his voice.

Benedict's eyes narrowed slightly, picking up on the subtle undercurrent. "Yes, that's right. I've been looking forward to meeting the man who keeps the supernatural order in Enchanted Springs." His words were courteous, but they carried a weight that suggested he was well aware of Jack's complex role in the paranormal community. "Your reputation as a mediator between the mystical and the mundane precedes you."

Jack's smile was tight but polite. "It seems we both have a keen interest in the secrets that lurk beneath the surface."

Benedict's expression flickered. "Perhaps. My inquiries might not involve a badge, but they require a certain... finesse in navigating the hidden corridors of our world. I understand you possess a unique talent for uncovering what prefers to remain hidden."

Jack's eyes narrowed slightly, his voice lowering to match the seriousness of Benedict's tone. "And I understand your investigations are quite prolific, delving into areas that many might think unsafe. It's a risky path, professor."

The air between the two men charged with a palpable tension, as if both were trying to gauge the other's intentions and strengths without giving away too much of their own.

Sadie, catching the intensity of their exchange, quickly intervened. "Gentlemen, tonight is about a fictional mystery, not an exploration of dark shadows and buried secrets."

Jack's gaze shifted briefly to Sadie, his expression softening before returning to Benedict with renewed resolve. "Of course. Tonight, we enjoy the festivities. But perhaps, professor, we might find a moment to discuss our shared interests further."

Benedict agreed with a cautious smile, his eyes sharp. "I would like that, detective. Understanding more about your methods could prove... enlightening."

Before the conversation could drift further, Violet did a little shimmy, almost as if she were already dancing to a song only she could hear. "I can hear the music starting already. Let's shake a leg, gang!"

"Don't you want to be fashionably late?"

She grinned, a mischievous sparkle in her translucent eyes. "I will be fashionably late, guaranteed. Ever since I died, I've had no other choice!" Her laughter tinkled through the shop like chimes in a gentle breeze.

I groaned at her bad play on words, though a smile tugged at my lips despite myself. "That's terrible, Violet," I said, but her infectious laughter made it impossible not to join in.

"Come on, everyone! Tonight's going to be one for the history books—or at least one for the blog." She winked at Sadie, who was still documenting everything on her smartphone.

With our spirits lifted by Violet's irrepressible charm, we gathered our things, ready to step out into the night and toward an evening that promised as much mirth as mystery.

CHAPTER 8

The Belmont Luxor Roadster

As we stepped out of the shop, the evening air was crisp and filled with anticipation. Parked at the curb was a stunning 1928 Belmont Luxor Roadster. The top was down, and its burgundy paint gleamed, promising a ride in classic style.

Sadie's mouth fell open in surprise. "Is this your car?"

Benedict ushered us toward the vehicle. "I borrowed it from a friend. After all, if we're going to drive into the Roaring Twenties, we might as well arrive in proper style."

He extended his arm in a welcoming gesture, then opened the passenger door for Sadie. She slid into the front seat with an appreciative sigh, while Jack helped me into the back seat, his hand light on my elbow.

The interior was every bit as luxurious as the exterior promised, with cream-colored upholstery and mahogany paneling. It felt more like a country club than a car.

Violet floated into the jump seat in the back, laughing. "I'll ride up here! It's the best view—and you know seating is optional for a gal like me."

As Benedict took the driver's seat, his hands settled comfortably on the wheel. The engine of the roadster roared to life, a smooth, rich sound that spoke of power and reliability. "Off we go." We pulled away from the curb, the car moving with a grace that belied its years.

Jack leaned closer to me, the leather seats creaking softly under his weight. His voice was low, almost a whisper, as he glanced briefly at Benedict's back before speaking. "It's a good thing you invited me tonight." His eyes met mine with a serious glint. "There's more going on here than meets the eye."

The roadster glided smoothly down Main Street, its engine purring softly, History seemed to pull closer, blurring the lines between the past and the present. Old-fashioned streetlights flickered to life, casting a gentle glow across sidewalks and storefronts. Flower baskets hung from wrought-iron lampposts, adding splashes of color to the scene.

We passed Buzzards' Roost, the local bar and grill, and a group of diners at a sidewalk table raised their glasses in salute. Their laughter was contagious, and we waved back joyfully in response. Benedict gave a friendly honk of the horn, its deep tone echoing down the street.

A bit further down the street, children chased each other across Courthouse Square, their cheerful shouts echoing through the air, while couples strolled hand-in-hand along the tree-lined pathways.

At the corner, the Parthenon Theater's grand marquee announced an upcoming play, its bold letters lighting up the night. The old building's classic brick façade and arched windows stood as proud reminders of the town's rich cultural heritage. Despite its growth over the years, Enchanted Springs had managed to retain its small-town charm—a community woven tightly with threads of history and a palpable sense of belonging. I often felt like Enchanted Springs seemed to exist in its own bubble, where the pace of life was gentle, and magic floated gently down every quiet street.

In the blink of an eye, we were at our destination. The Lydia Hotel loomed over us, a towering relic that cast an eerie silhouette against the darkening sky. A century ago, it had been a beacon of elegance and prosperity. Now it looked more like a haunted house than a grand hotel.

The parking lot was deserted, weeds clawing their way through cracks in the asphalt. The lower-level windows were boarded up. Broken windows on the upper floors stared out blankly, like the empty eye sockets of a long-forgotten skull, witnessing the passage of time without a glance.

The lush gardens that once surrounded the hotel were overgrown, flowerbeds and manicured hedges replaced by wild shrubs and tangled weeds.

The grand entrance, where limousines and carriages once paused to drop off well-heeled guests, was quiet. Ornate front doors, once thrown open in welcome, were chained and locked, I wondered if the barricades were meant to keep intruders out—or keep secrets in.

The contrast between the hotel's lively past and its ghostly present was palpable. The air around the building felt thicker, heavier, as if weighed down by the layers of dust and shadows.

My heart sank. I couldn't hide my disappointment, and I groaned in dismay. "What a wreck."

Sadie sighed. "It seemed so much nicer in my imagination."

For the last few days, we had been swept up in the excitement of dressing up and stepping out for the evening, expecting to find the old hotel transformed back to its former glory. Instead, the dilapidated building that greeted us wasn't even close to the sparkling venue we had imagined.

Sadie turned around in her seat to look at me. "I can't believe this. It looks even worse close up than it does from the street. Are we really supposed to go in there?"

I nodded in agreement, equally disheartened. "This isn't at all what I expected. How could anyone host a party in that place?"

From the driver's seat, Benedict spoke, his expression serious. "I must admit, I'm concerned about the structural integrity of this place. It looks as though a stiff breeze could knock it over. No evening of entertainment is worth risking our lives."

But then, beside me, Jack chuckled. "Just give it a moment."

Violet leaned toward me. "Look again, Red."

As I turned back to the hotel, the air in front of us seemed to ripple like the surface of a disturbed pond. A shimmering, radiant wave of energy swept over the parking lot, enveloping us in a warm, golden glow. I blinked, and in the next moment, the derelict hotel transformed before our eyes.

The peeling paint and boarded-up windows were replaced by gleaming white walls and polished panes of glass. Lights twinkled invitingly from every window, casting a warm welcome that beckoned us inside. The overgrown lawn was now a carpet of manicured grass, with a herd of topiary shrubs carved into the shapes lions, elephants, and giraffes. Masses of hydrangeas and roses bloomed in English gardens, their colors vibrant under the starlit sky.

The parking lot was bustling with activity, filled with vintage automobiles of the 1920s, each one gleaming under the street-lamps. Valets in crisp uniforms moved efficiently around the grand entrance, greeting guests as dozens of well-dressed patrons made their way inside. The sound of jazz and laughter spilled out into the night air.

The transformation was complete and utterly magical. I turned to Violet for an explanation. "How did they do that?"

She replied with a single word. "Magic."

Jack explained further. "It's been warded—shielded, essentially, to mask it from the eyes of ordinary people passing by. It's sort of a supernatural security system."

Benedict laughed and waxed professorial. "Of course! A potent veil of glamour cloaks the Lydia Hotel, rendering it invisible to the unenchanted eye. Where outsiders see dilapidation, those touched by magic see a gem of the night hidden in plain sight."

A battalion of valets in matching wool coats converged on us in a choreographed dance of courtesy and efficiency, opening the doors of the roadster. One of them extended a gloved hand to help me out of the car. I felt like a celebrity. A phantom valet attended to Violet, who floated down from the rumble seat like a starlet at a movie premiere.

In the blink of an eye, Jack was at my side. He offered his arm, and I took it, my heart racing with anticipation as we joined the stream of guests gliding into the radiant warmth of the revived Lydia Hotel.

CHAPTER 9

We've Been Expecting You

W E FOLLOWED THE RED carpet to the grand entrance, where two massive Art Deco doors stood open. As we stepped through, we were greeted by a uniformed maître 'd' in a dark, double-breasted coat.

With a courteous tip of his cap, he ushered us in. "Good evening, friends. We've been expecting you." And then, to top it off, he welcomed us by name. "A pleasure to see you again, Detective Edgewood. Mrs. Serrano, you're looking vibrant as always. And this must be the rest of your ensemble: Professor Sadie Arragon, Professor Benedict Cumberland, and of course Miss Marley Montgomery." His eyebrows raised slightly when he looked at me. "If you don't mind my saying so, you bear a strong resemblance to your grandmother Clara. Beauty runs in the family."

"Thank you." My curiosity was piqued. "It seems you know quite a bit about us."

He simply nodded. "Our staff takes pride in serving our guests to the utmost. What kind of hosts would we be if we didn't even know your names?" He gestured grandly across the lobby. "Please, the main event awaits you through those doors. The night is young, and the revelries are just beginning."

We followed a steady stream of guests heading toward the party. On the way, a man in a shiny black suit stepped forward to shake Jack's hand. I noticed the badge on his lapel: Eddie Hawkner, Chief Security Officer.

"Jack, my friend, you look like you're on edge. Relax, tonight's on me. I've got everything under control."

Jack offered a polite nod, his expression softening slightly. "I appreciate that, Eddie."

"Of course." Eddie's gaze flickered briefly across the room before settling back on Jack. "Enjoy the evening. After all, that's what I'm here for. While I'm on duty, everyone can forget their troubles for a few hours."

Our steps echoed softly on the polished marble as we made our way across the lobby and into the speakeasy we'd heard so much about.

The air inside was perfumed with the scent of fresh flowers and the smoky sweet aroma of distilled spirits. Crystal chandeliers cast a sparkling light over the crowd.

Sadie leaned in, her eyes sparkling with excitement. "Can you believe this place? It's like stepping back in time!"

Violet nodded enthusiastically. "It's exactly like the old days—except for one thing." She elbowed Jack. "We used to hide from lawmen like you. Now it's all out in the open."

As soon as we stepped into *Spirits*, the swell of an unearthly melody enveloped us. Before I could even scan the opulent décor of the club, my gaze was drawn irresistibly to the stage. There, materializing from wisps of silvery mist, was an orchestra. Not just any orchestra, either. These magicians were specters, each ghostly figure clad in the dazzling attire of the 1920s. Men in sharp tailcoats and women in shimmering flapper dresses held their instruments high, with an eerie enthusiasm that matched the spirited music they played.

The band leader was a dapper figure with slicked-back hair and a baton that glowed. His movements were fluid, almost floating, as if he were conducting not just the music but the very air around him. "Look at that," Sadie's voice was tinged with awe. "It's like they're straight out of the Cotton Club."

The room itself responded to their tunes. Shadows on the walls danced and the chandeliers above flickered rhythmically, as if they were applauding.

The brass section, a trio of ghostly figures with trombones and trumpets, played with a passion that seemed to pierce the veil between worlds, their notes lingering sweetly in the air.

At the grand piano, a woman with bobbed hair poured her soul into the keys, her transparent fingers moving so swiftly they were almost a blur. Each note she struck was like a greeting from the past, echoing through the crowded room and sending chills of appreciation through the crowd.

I couldn't help but be drawn in by the ethereal spectacle. The music, the ghostly musicians—it was a hauntingly beautiful performance that seemed to bend the very fabric of reality.

"Do you think they know they're still playing, after all these years?" I asked, turning to Jack, who was watching the stage with a mixture of fascination and something that looked suspiciously like professional curiosity.

"They might not," he replied softly. "Or perhaps this is exactly what they choose to do—play forever in a loop of their happiest moments. Either way, it's captivating."

Captivating was an understatement. As the band swung into a particularly lively jazz number, the whole room seemed to pulse with energy. Couples drifted toward the dance floor, their movements smooth and practiced, as if the music itself guided their steps.

It was a moment suspended in time, a perfect bubble of the past that had somehow survived into the present. And as I watched the phantom band play on, I felt a connection to the revelry and despair of the era they represented, a touching reminder of the thin line between joy and sorrow.

I looked around, astounded at the décor. Art Deco fixtures cast geometric patterns across the gilded walls. Velvet chairs were grouped around small, intimate tables, and a long bar stretched across the far end of the room, its surface gleaming under the soft lighting.

The atmosphere was electric with the buzz of conversations and the soft clinking of glasses. Small groups of people mingled, exchanging pleasantries and laughter, raising their glasses in cheerful toasts as they admired each other's outfits. Women wore beaded and embroidered evening gowns that sparkled under the soft lighting. Most wore pearls and gemstones to accentuate their dresses. Some wore jeweled headbands, like Violet, or feathered fascinators in their hair. Men, not to be outdone, sported sharp suits and tuxedos, some with pinstripes, others in solid, somber tones.

Meanwhile, handsome waiters glided through the room, carrying a dazzling array of Prohibition-era cocktails. One approached us with a silver platter of beverages, accompanied by hand-lettered placards for each.

I didn't know where to start. "They all look so good—even the ones I've never heard of."

Violet's eyes twinkled mischievously as she glanced around our little group. "How about a little game? I'll match each of you with a Prohibition cocktail that suits your personality."

I shrugged. Why not let a long-dead flapper ply us with alcohol? What could go wrong?

CHAPTER 10

Here's to Your Health

VIOLET STARTED WITH JACK. "For you, detective, the obvious choice might seem like the Manhattan, given its bold and classic nature. However..." She paused, giving him a more scrutinizing look. "Tonight calls for something a bit more adventurous: a Negroni. The drink of Italian counts. And as luck would have it, the negronis here at *Spirits* are garnished with sections of blood orange."

Jack raised an eyebrow and nodded. "An excellent choice."

Next, Violet turned to Sadie. "For our esteemed professor of history, I'd recommend the French 75. It's intellectual, potent, and has a celebratory flair—much like your lectures, in and out of the classroom."

Sadie's eyes sparkled with anticipation as she picked up a slender flute filled with the bubbly golden liquid. She took a small sip and sighed. "Like Dom Pérignon used to say, 'I have tasted stars.' But there's a hint of something extra... a bit of magic in the bubbles, maybe?"

When Violet's gaze landed on me, she hummed thoughtfully. "Marley, you're an interesting blend of sweet, sour—and spirited." She laughed at her own joke. "I'd say the Clover Club is the perfect aperitif for you. It's elegant, a bit understated, and has layers of flavor waiting to be discovered, like the mysteries you love to unravel."

I couldn't disagree. "Well, I'll have one, but then I'll switch to ginger ale. I'm not sure I want to let my guard down around so many paranormals. I'm not sure how trustworthy everyone is."

Jack put a reassuring hand on my back. "Don't worry. I know almost everybody here, and you'll be safe with me."

Violet waved her hand as she dismissed my concern. "Ah, Red, you won't get tipsy at *Spirits*. The drinks they serve here aren't your typical cocktails."

That sounded ominous, actually. I suddenly felt even more worried about the drink I held in my hand.

She gestured toward the bar where a waiter was serving a tray of iridescent drinks that seemed to glow softly in the dim light. "Nothing here is alcoholic. As Sadie guessed, they're imbued with a bit of magic. Each sip brings a wave of happiness, enough to make you feel calm and relaxed, but without the pesky side effects of poisoning your liver."

Sadie took another sip of her French 75. "I knew it! This is too good to be ordinary champagne."

Violet nodded enthusiastically. "It's part of what makes *Spirits* so unique. Lucius insists on it. He believes that true relaxation comes from innate joy, not inebriation."

Violet stroked her chin thoughtfully as she considered the remaining drinks that servers were passing on silver trays. "Now, Professor Cumberwell. The Sidecar has been popular since the

Great War. Cognac, orange liqueur, lemon juice. If I had to guess, I'd say that's your drink."

He tilted his head, considering. "I'd put it in my top three."

"I'm a pretty quick study, professor. And now for yours truly. Let me think... Am I in the mood for a cool and refreshing mint julep, a tropical Mary Pickford, or a sweet and sassy bee's knees? Hmmm. Maybe one of each!"

She reached for a mint julep and lifted the frosted silver cup to her lips, her spectral hand solidifying just enough to grasp it. I couldn't hide my astonishment. "Violet, you can actually hold it?"

With a sly grin, she took a delicate sip, savoring the taste. "Oh, my dear, everything in *Spirits* is enchanted. I thought you knew that. Lucius takes it as a point of pride that all of his guests can live it up—even if we're dead."

"But how?"

Violet held her glass up, beaming. "I guess it's not that hard to explain. Noncorporeal beings like me can enjoy food and drinks that have been lightly sprinkled with Moonshadow Mother-of-Pearl Dust. Lucius imports it to ensure that non-corporeal guests can enjoy every dish at a his gatherings."

Sadie stammered in surprise. "I thought that was just a legend!"

Violet chuckled, taking another sip. "It's no myth, darling. But it's exceedingly rare. The dust is derived from pearls that have absorbed moonlight for an entire lunar cycle. Mesmerizing nymphs harvest these pearls from the depths of enchanted seas—supposedly, only during a blue moon, which adds to its scarcity."

She winked, her tone playful. "And trust me, getting nymphs to part with their treasures? It's like trying to steal a song from a siren!"

CHAPTER 11

Party Like It's 1899

A T A NEARBY TABLE, a young woman in a dress with shimmering sequins leaned close to her companion. "Did you hear about the Thompsons' séance last week?" she whispered, her voice tinged with excitement. "They say they contacted Houdini himself. Can you imagine?"

Her friend shifted slightly in his seat, and I noticed that his entire body was covered with hair. A werewolf! In public! Despite the fact that he was more monster than man, his voice was low and smooth, with a hint of a French accent. "In Florida, I'd believe almost anything. But let's hope Houdini shared some of his escape tricks. We might need them if this night gets any wilder."

To my left, a group of elderly gentlemen in matching red jackets discussed something with earnest intensity. "It's all about ley lines," one insisted, tapping a finger on the tabletop for emphasis. "They intersect right under the hotel, you know. Gives the place its paranormal properties."

His friend, a tall man with an air of scholarly detachment, nodded thoughtfully. "Indeed, it amplifies spiritual activity.

Makes *Spirits* a hotspot for our kind—both the present, and the dearly departed."

As I took another sip of my Clover Club, the nearby laughter and clinking of glasses drew my attention to a man who was describing other dances he remembered. "Nothing compares to the New Year's Eve gala of 1899. Imagine welcoming the twentieth century in this very room, at the dawn of the Edison era. The atmosphere was *literally* electric. We felt like we were living in the future!"

Yes, I might be eavesdropping, but the stories I was hearing were blowing my mind. At the table next to ours, an vampire in a purple tuxedo spoke nostalgically of a masquerade ball held in Venice in the 1600s. He gestured around the room. "Every immortal needs a respite from eternity. Events like these are the only way of keeping the centuries from blurring into a monotonous march."

Benedict leaned in slightly toward our table. "It's true. Gatherings like this one are steeped in tradition. Centuries ago, Count Henri de Montclair hosted a masquerade ball in a secluded chateau in the heart of Paris. His chateau was aglow with enchanted lanterns, casting eerie shadows that danced along with the guests. Vampires, witches, even a couple of ancient spirits mingled, sharing tales of centuries passed. It was a night to remember, breaking the ennui that often accompanies immortal life."

Next to me, Sadie chimed in, her historian's interest piqued. "I've also read about the ghostly gatherings of the 1800s in New Orleans. Spirits of the departed would converge on the old plantations, drawn by the music of lost souls, to dance until the day broke."

Benedict nodded appreciatively. "Exactly, Sadie. These gatherings serve as a reminder of our shared histories, our collective memories. They're a chance to feel alive, to connect with our kind, and to celebrate the enduring magic of our existence."

As our little group enjoyed the lively buzz, two figures approached. The man was tall and dark, in a brocade tuxedo jacket with a velvet lapel. I wondered for a moment if he was a shifter—a panther, perhaps. Then he smiled, and I noticed the tell-tale glint of his incisors. He was a vampire, like Jack. But while Jack's eyes sparkled with humanity, this man's gaze was dark and inscrutable.

Beside him, a woman with flowing black tresses glided across the floor. Her sequined red gown clung to her like a second skin, casting fireworks around the room. Her beauty was striking. So was the smile that curved on her lips as she surveyed the assembly.

Sadie leaned toward me and whispered in my ear. "Marley, who's that?"

Before I could answer, the man stopped directly in front of us, his companion's gaze flickering over me with an intensity that made me clutch my drink a little tighter.

CHAPTER 12

The Charmer and the Chanteuse

I'M NOT GOING TO lie. They scared me a little.

The man narrowed his eyes as he approached and squared his shoulders. I cringed when I saw him raise his fist. My breath caught when he swung it toward Jack—but then Jack met the newcomer's fist with his own, connecting in an energetic mid-air bump.

Both men were grinning ear to ear. In the next moment, they pulled each other into a big, rough hug, thumping each other's backs in a show of genuine camaraderie.

The tuxedoed man stepped back, still smiling broadly, perfect white teeth framed by a matching pair of dimples. "Jack, I hope you left your badge at home. Tonight's all about drama, not danger."

Jack's response was quick and tinged with dry humor. "You know me. I don't mind a little bloodshed, as long as it's all in good fun."

Jack turned toward me. "Marley, allow me to introduce Lucius Black, the man behind the mystery at *Spirits*. Lucius, this is Marley Montgomery, the new proprietor of the Enchanted Antique Shop."

Lucius reached forward and gently kissed the back of my hand. A chill ran down my spine. I didn't know if the cause was his old-world charm, or if his touch had been a subtle way to scan my magical ability.

"Welcome, Marley! I've heard a bit about you. Your charming grandmother and her delightful friend Eleanor are in the kitchen even as we speak, conjuring their magical patisseries."

Violet greeted Lucius with an ethereal air kiss. "Mr. Black, you've outdone yourself. I've never seen *Spirits* looking more festive."

Lucius's smile broadened. "Ah, my darling Violet. No party is complete without you."

As the laughter from their greeting settled, Violet glided forward with her usual flair. "Meet the rest of our little circle. This is Sadie Arragon and her friend, Benedict Cumberwell." Then she introduced us to the striking woman beside Lucius. "This vision in silver is Calypso, the resident songstress here at *Spirits*." She turned eagerly toward her. "You will be singing tonight, won't you?"

Calypso's nod was regal, her smile enigmatic. "Of course. But I'll also be performing a small part in our little play."

Lucius's gaze shifted to Benedict, a subtle change flickered across his expression. "Dr. Cumberwell, your reputation precedes you. A scholar of the dark arts is always an intriguing addition to our gatherings. I trust your insights tonight will be... illuminating."

Benedict offered a polite nod, his smile tight but courteous. "I'm here to enjoy the festivities, Lucius. The academic in me is off duty. Well, mostly off duty."

Lucius chuckled, easing the momentary tension. "We must chat about the magical artifacts you've encountered."

Calypso leaned forward toward me. "Speaking of artifacts, where did you find that mesmerizing necklace? That ruby, those pearls... they're exquisite! They're far more gorgeous than this prop necklace I'm wearing for the murder mystery tonight."

She raised an elegant hand to the necklace around her neck. It was beautiful, but I had to admit, it paled in comparison to mine. A ruby solitaire dangled gracefully from a delicate gold chain, accented by a single lustrous pearl. It was elegant, but it was hardly a showstopper.

I touched my necklace, feeling the glass stones underneath my fingertips. "It's only costume jewelry," I replied modestly.

"Well, it puts my necklace to shame. Lucius, darling, why couldn't we have found a piece like that for tonight's performance?"

Calypso's playful complaint drew a chuckle from Lucius, who gave her a consoling pat on the shoulder. "Ah, Calypso, you're the only gem we need on stage. No diamonds or pearls could compare to your own natural beauty," he teased.

I found myself making an impulsive offer. "That's true. But if you'd like, you could borrow my necklace for the show. I wouldn't mind."

The offer seemed to delight Calypso as much as her compliment had flattered me. Her face lit up, a smile of genuine surprise and delight spreading across her features. "Would you really lend it to me? Oh, it would be perfect for my part! I think my character could use a touch more glamour."

I nodded, unclasping the necklace and holding it out to her. "Absolutely. It's all in good fun, right?"

Calypso reached for the necklace, her fingers brushing mine as she accepted my offer. "Thank you, Marley. This is incredibly kind of you. I promise to take the utmost care of it."

As Calypso held the necklace in her hands, her expression transformed into one of professional admiration. She carefully studied each jewel, her eyes tracing the craftsmanship with the discernment of a connoisseur. "Look at these rubies," she exclaimed, holding the necklace up to the light. "The cut is exquisite—see how each facet catches the light, creating a fiery dance within the stones? And these diamonds," she continued, her finger gently caressing the smaller stones set between the rubies, "are brilliant cuts, the true stars of the jeweler's art."

I thought she was going a bit overboard for costume jewelry, but whatever. Maybe she was a method actor.

Just as she was about to drape my necklace around her neck, she paused and looked at me thoughtfully. "Oh, but if I wear your necklace, you'll be unadorned. Not that you need any adornment with that beautiful face." She smiled warmly, her compliment making me blush. "But here. Let me lend you my necklace for the evening."

I was touched by her gesture. "Thank you, Calypso. This is beautiful."

As Calypso slipped the solitaire around my neck, Benedict leaned in, his voice low and tinged with intrigue. "Both pieces are more than simply beautiful, Marley. All jewelry, once worn, carries echoes of the wearer. Sometimes they share secrets you don't expect."

Calypso nodded in agreement, her eyes reflecting the flicker of candlelight. "Indeed, every gem has its own story—but tonight, our story will be one of mystery and wonder!"

As Calypso continued to run her fingers over the pearls around her neck, her expression turned thoughtful, almost conspiratorial. "You know, there's another reason I was so taken with this piece." Her voice dropped as if she was sharing a secret. "It will play a crucial role in tonight's murder mystery drama."

"Really? How so?"

Calypso's eyes sparkled with excitement. "Let's just say that a ruby necklace—a magical piece of jewelry known as the 'Crimson Teardrop'—is the key to unlocking the mystery we're about to enact. It's integral to the plot. I think your necklace adds a layer of authenticity—and perhaps a bit of real magic—to our drama."

Lucius raised his glass to me. "To Marley, for her generous spirit," he declared. The rest joined in the toast, and for a moment, the air was filled with the clinking of glasses and good wishes.

As the excitement began to settle, Lucius's voice once again captured the attention of the room. "Speaking of tonight's drama," he announced with a flourish, "it's almost time for the performance to begin."

A sudden, clear chime resonated throughout the ballroom, its celestial tone cutting through the din with an ethereal clarity. Lucius stood. "Ah," he remarked, straightening his tuxedo coat. "It begins."

The candles on the tables sputtered as if caught in a draft that no one could feel. A soft, almost imperceptible gasp echoed through the room.

Lucius paused, a slight smile playing on his lips as if he relished the momentary suspense. "Shall we see what the evening holds for us?"

The crowd was captivated, waiting for what would come next. He finally broke the dramatic silence with a grand gesture toward a pair of double doors. A celestial chord echoed through the air, and the doors flew open to reveal a palatial ballroom.

"Please, follow me."

Everyone's attention was riveted on Lucius, but my gaze was drawn toward Calypso. As she turned to accompany him, the dim lighting caught something unsettling—a fleeting shadow that didn't align with her movements, a dark silhouette merging with her own, only to vanish as quickly as it appeared.

I blinked, half-expecting the shadow to reappear. But it was gone, leaving only a lingering sense of dread that tightened around my chest.

"Did anyone else see that?" I looked around, but my voice was lost in the gathering crowd.

CHAPTER 13

Beneath the Ballroom Lights

JACK OFFERED ME HIS arm, and Benedict offered his arm to Sadie, and we all followed Lucius and Calypso into the ballroom.

The space had been transformed into an opulent dining room, with tables draped in pristine linen, glinting with candle-light and floral centerpieces.

"Marley, look at those flowers!" Sadie pointed to an arrangement of deep red roses and delicate baby's breath. "Aren't they gorgeous?"

I nodded, my attention drawn past the flowers to Calypso. She was circulating among the guests, sipping champagne from a crystal flute. From this distance, her striking features seemed hidden behind an eerie mist, half-obscured by a wispy fog that seemed to cling to her and her alone. I blinked, and the mist was gone. Maybe I had only seen a puff of smoke from one of the hundreds of candles in the room.

I reassured myself that it was an optical illusion. Calypso was fine, I was fine, everyone in the room was fine. Yes, I had recently discovered my ability to see spirits and brief flashes of the past, but this was neither of those things. I told myself to take a deep breath and relax.

At one end of the ballroom, a stage draped in rich red velvet curtains promised entertainment and surprises yet to come. Violet, who had been floating along ahead of us, waved us over to one of the tables. "Check this out, gang! We're here, front and center near the stage."

Our table, set for six, was positioned with a clear view of the dais, guaranteeing us a front-row seats for the evening's entertainment.

Each seat at the table featured place cards with our names hand-lettered in calligraphic swirls. I picked mine up. I couldn't tell if the ink was black or dark crimson.

I have to admit that I've been to weddings and events where the place cards put me in uncomfortable proximity to people I didn't like—but tonight, I was happy to see that I'd be seated between Jack and Sadie. Violet would sit on Jack's right, while Benedict would be on Sadie's left.

One detail that tugged at my heartstrings, though, was the empty chair beside Violet. It had been reserved for a certain Victor Serrano.

In my short time back in Enchanted Springs, Violet rarely mentioned her husband. I was certain, though, that they must have been reunited. Even if he'd lived to a ripe old age, he surely would have crossed over into the Spirit World years ago.

As we took our seats, excited chatter filled the room, each guest eagerly discussing their expectations for the night. Some speculated about the roles their friends were playing. Others admired the attention to detail that Lucius had poured into the setting. The atmosphere was electric, buzzing with the energy of guests, their laughter and conversations creating a lively hum.

Nearby, I noticed Madame Endora, one of my grandmother's friends, and her spirit guide Consuela. Normally, Consuela wasn't visible to anyone but Endora, but tonight she was laughing and chatting like any other partygoer, her shimmering silhouette flickering like candlelight in the dimly lit room.

I scanned the room and spotted a few more familiar faces. There was Mr. Pennington, an enigmatic collector whose passion for Tiffany lamps had led him to my shop on several occasions. He caught my eye and nodded, his mustache twitching in a semblance of a smile. Beside him sat Mrs. Pennington. Last year, she had acquired a Victorian-era mirror from me, one that reputedly belonged to the Empress Eugenie of France.

Sadie gasped when she saw Mrs. Pennington's dress. "Did you notice the detailing on that gown? It's a perfect replica of a 1925 Jeanne Lanvin. See the geometric patterns? They're a hallmark of the Art Deco influence on fashion."

Violet craned her neck to see. "Wowza. That's not a replica, either. Those Penningtons are loaded." Then she spelled it out, to clarify: "R-I-C-H."

I admired the dress, but my attention soon drifted to the crystal stemware on our table. "Look at these," I gestured to Sadie, picking up a wine glass. "Fostoria Chintz crystal. These were very popular in the early twentieth century." I turned the stemware it in my hand to admire the intricate floral design etched into the bowl of each glass. "This isn't something you see every day—unless, of course, you own an antique shop."

Just then, a passing gentleman in a crisp pinstripe suit chimed in. "I couldn't help but overhear." His voice carried the faint trace of an English accent. "If you'll notice, all of the place settings are extraordinary. The silverware, for example, isn't silver—it's white gold. In an abundance of caution, it's designed to ensure that no magical beings are harmed, particularly those who might be allergic."

I must have looked confused because Benedict leaned forward to explain. "Fairies, werewolves, demons—some of them find themselves quite incapacitated by silver. Even vampires, ghosts, and witches, if I may be so bold, can be unpleasantly affected." He glanced around with a mischievous smile. "I do hope no one at this table is adversely impacted by an accidental glance of adamantium."

Jack reached for a carafe of sparkling water and grunted. "I think we're good here, Benny."

Sadie looked delighted by the information, her eyes scanning the room with renewed appreciation. I, on the other hand, felt a sudden realization dawning on me. Glancing around at the crowd, many of whom exhibited unusual traits, I said the quiet part out loud. "I think there might be more paranormal people in Enchanted Springs than I realized."

Violet's expression turned slightly more somber, her voice lowering to a whisper that carried a weight of hidden truths. "That's only the surface, Marley. Creatures from the darkest corners of Florida are drawn here. *Spirits* isn't just a haven—it's a crossroads."

Benedict nodded, his eyes scanning the room as if looking for hidden dangers. "Indeed, and you know what they say about crossroads—they're places where deals are struck with forces unseen, where paths to hidden fates intersect. Tread carefully, for the choices you make here can change the future."

CHAPTER 14

You Can't Tell the Players without a Program

J ACK SIGHED AND POURED water for Violet and me, then passed the pitcher to Benedict, who filled Sadie's glass. While everyone settled in, I picked up one of the programs that had been left at each place.

The cover of the program was made from thick, textured cream paper, soft to the touch but sturdy, with a subtle iridescent sheen that caught the light. The event's title, "The Crimson Heist," was prominently embossed in scarlet ink, with a touch of gold leaf that highlighted the elegant, swirling font. The programs were tied with red satin ribbon to match the colored text.

I carefully untied the ribbon and opened the program to the first page, which detailed the evening's menu. Each course was described in mouthwatering detail: Smoked Salmon and Caviar Blini, Truffled Cauliflower Soup, Roasted Beet and Goat Cheese Salad, and Beef Wellington with Madeira Sauce. My grandmother's desserts—Chocolate Ganache Tart and Sour Orange Pie—promised a sweet conclusion to the meal.

The next section introduced the cast of "The Crimson Heist." I read them aloud, and Jack and Sadie offered commentary.

"Lucius Black as the evening's emcee," I said, my finger trailing down the list. "Well, he's our host, so that makes sense. And look, Calypso Colbert is playing the model at the auction."

I continued, moving down the list. "Here's something intriguing. Who is Frankie 'Fingers' Flynn?"

Violet guffawed. "Seriously? Talk about your typecasting. He got that nickname because he was the smoothest pickpocket in town. When he wasn't stealing from guys on the street, he was helping himself to a five-finger discount in all the shops. He used to be the best-known pickpocket in Florida."

Jack smiled. "I remember him. Frankie practically had his own cell at the county jail. He must have gone on the straight and narrow after he crossed over, because he hasn't been in any trouble since the day he died."

We all laughed. In a social setting like this, Jack was actually funny. Who knew?

I turned my attention back to the program. "Next up, Serena Severina as a socialite, and Alex Trenholm as the charming auctioneer."

Violet looked at Jack, who nodded thoughtfully. "It's a role that suits him, don't you think?" She turned back to Sadie and me. "Wait until you see this guy. He's a real sweet talker."

I continued. "Glen Goldman as a raconteur, and Cora Fay as an enchantress."

Violet's laughter was soft but genuine. "Art imitating life, or is it the other way around?"

Since I didn't know any of them, I guess I would wait to find out.

"And finally, Jasmine Bloom as a jewel collector and Tommy Tucker as a security guard."

Violent simply shrugged. "Meh."

I turned to the synopsis of the performance. "According to this, the evening is set around a high-stakes auction where the Crimson Teardrop ruby goes missing after a sudden blackout. And it seems everyone has a motive." I laughed, touching the borrowed gemstone at my neck. "Well, if they're looking for this particular necklace, I might be their main suspect."

I laid the program down. The room buzzed with anticipation. All around me, people were discussing the show. "Looks like we're in for quite the evening," I said to Sadie, who nodded in agreement.

A waiter approached us with a tray of hors d'oeuvres, bowing as he announced his offering: Mini Lobster Thermidor Tartlets. With a polite smile and a pair of golden tongs, he deftly served each of us a delicate pastry brimming with rich, creamy lobster.

I bit into mine. The pastry melted in my mouth, and the flavors danced on my palate. The rich, creamy texture of the lobster mingled seamlessly with the subtle sharpness of Parmesan cheese. I think I might have moaned a little too loudly, because Violet immediately said, "I'll have what she's having."

I rolled my eyes at her, then turned to Sadie. "Do these have a hint of mustard?"

Sadie nodded in agreement. "Fancy Dijon mustard. Sylvia outdoes herself every time."

Sylvia Robinson was practically a legend in Enchanted Springs. For years, she had owned and operated Southern Comfort Catering, where she specialized in family friendly favorites like barbecue and briskets. Recently, she had expanded her line to include even more menu items and a broader clientele.

Once again, I looked around the bustling room, noting the oddities in some guests' appearances and mannerisms. "Wait a minute. Is everyone here paranormal in some way? Even the servers?"

Sadie shrugged. "It looks that way. Why?"

"Because the only thing magical about Sylvia is her cooking. She must be freaking out."

"Well, if I had to guess, I'd say Lucius probably cast a subtle spell—let's call it a 'hospitality hex'—to make Sylvia believe she's simply catering another high-profile event. She might think it's an eccentric pop up. It's all very enchanting to her, literally."

As we savored the last bites of lobster, the room's attention suddenly shifted. Calypso was gliding toward our table.

"The necklace I am wearing," Calypso began, her voice smooth and enticing, drawing the room into a hushed anticipation, "is truly one of a kind. Not only for its physical beauty, but for the enchantment it carries." She delicately touched the necklace draped elegantly around her neck—my necklace— but clearly she was in character as the auctioneer's model.

"Note how the stones catch the light and shimmer with an ethereal glow."

She wasn't joking. As she moved, the ruby pendant seemed to pulse with a life of its own, casting a soft luminescence that drew gasps from everyone watching.

"Observe the way the light dances within the gems," Calypso purred, her eyes glinting with excitement. "It's as if they hold a bit of Venusian magic."

She was standing right next to me, so I could see the necklace clearly. I had handled it back at the shop, thinking it was nothing more than well-crafted costume jewelry. Yet here, in the glow of Calypso's charismatic presentation, the necklace did more than sparkle; it vibrated in a dance of fiery light.

What if I'd been mistaken? What if the necklace wasn't some old costume jewelry stashed in the storage room? What if it was real?

I wasn't a jewelry expert. I didn't know how to tell the difference between glass beads and pearls, much less between colored glass and rubies. I couldn't distinguish between diamonds and cubic zirconium. Sure, we had a device to test diamonds at the shop, but in my enthusiasm, I hadn't bothered to check. I'd made an assumption—a thoughtless guess. And in my careless naivete, I realized that my supposition could even be dangerous. If the "Crimson Teardrop" was real, that meant it could be enchanted, too.

Could actual magic be woven into those stones?

I leaned slightly closer to Sadie. "Does the necklace look different to you now? In the shop, it seemed simple... Now, I'm not so sure."

Sadie nodded, her eyes also focused on the necklace. "Magic has a way of revealing itself under the right light."

The murmur of the crowd grew as Calypso continued to enchant them with the necklace's lore and beauty, setting the stage for what was to come next in the evening's planned drama—the imaginary auction.

I remembered Benedict's words about jewelry holding the essence of its wearer. His warning hung in the air, lending an eerie weight to the evening's frivolity. As I pondered its possible significance, the band struck up a lively tune, momentarily dispelling the gathering shadows of my thoughts. Yet, the sensation of being at a crossroads, with unseen forces weaving through the crowded room, worried me.

Calypso drifted past our table once more. She paused, seemingly caught in a moment of contemplation, her fingertips gently touching the gem at her throat. Her expression was a mixture of reverence and resolve.

Sadie was captivated. "She's perfect for the part."

I nodded, unable to shake the feeling that there was more to Calypso's role tonight than mere performance.

As if he was reading my mind, Jack leaned toward me. "She's no ordinary performer. Keep an eye on her. The way she navigates the crowd, the subtle exchanges—there's a play within the play tonight."

His advice struck a chord with me as I watched Calypso merge back into the flow of the party, her figure a fleeting shadow among the glittering guests. My curiosity piqued, I resolved to keep an eye on her, wondering what secrets the night would unveil.

CHAPTER 15

Old Flames, New Fires

MY MOMENT OF QUIET contemplation was short-lived.

From the fringes of the room, a swarthy figure with a rogue's charm sauntered toward our table. He was dressed like a dandy from the Roaring Twenties—white dinner jacket, slicked-back hair, and a rakish fedora tilted at a daring angle. He might have been wearing a costume for the show, but he had the air of a man who thrived on mischief. His eyes sparkled with a mischievous glint as he plopped down in the chair next to Violet.

"Violet, toots, you are a sight for sore eyes! Where ya been, dollface? I've missed you around these parts." He grinned, a wide, open-mouthed smile that revealed a gold front tooth.

Violet rolled her eyes. "The feeling isn't mutual, Frankie. I don't remember inviting you to pull up a chair."

"A gentleman like me needs no invitation. We're all friends here, ain't we?" He swiveled his head around the table, his grin widening. "I just haven't met all of you yet. My name is Frankie, but my friends call me 'Fingers.'"

Without waiting for introductions, he reached across the table and helped himself to the last lobster appetizer on my plate. "And now that we've broken bread together, I think it's safe to say that I can count you all among my closest personal acquaintances."

Violet snorted. "Yeah, Frankie. We're thick as thieves."

He nodded appreciatively and turned his charm toward Sadie. "You look like a goddess tonight. Jean Harlow would pale in comparison to you."

He put his elbow on the table and grinned lasciviously.

He might have looked ordinary enough to an outsider, but there was a slyness about him that put me on guard. I wasn't alone. In the next instant, Jack's hand shot out, catching Frankie's wrist and twisting it roughly. A small, shiny object tumbled from Frankie's grasp—Violet's earring.

Frankie chuckled, rubbing his wrist theatrically. "Hold on there, ya' dirty copper! Talk about your police brutality!" He held both hands up as if he was surrendering. "No harm done, detective. Just making sure you're all paying attention!" He winked at us, his demeanor unshaken by the encounter. "It's all part of the act, folks. All in good fun!"

As Frankie moved on to charm another table, laughing as he went, another figure approached us. Like all the players in tonight's performance, the amateur actors were circulating, engaging guests in playful chit-chat that added to the night's mysterious allure.

Violet's eyes narrowed slightly as she recognized the incoming performer. "Ugh. Here comes Serena Severina."

"The socialite?"

Violet sneered. "More like 'parasite.' If you thought Frankie was something, brace yourself. She won't be happy until she's filched your secrets—and your man."

Serena Severina swept toward our table, her every step a calculated glide that seemed choreographed to captivate. She was dressed to kill, draped in a shimmering gold lamé dress that clung to her curves and flowed like liquid metal with each step she took. The dress featured an intricate beaded collar that mimicked the style of an ancient Egyptian pharaoh, regal and commanding.

Around her upper arms, serpent bangles coiled gracefully, their emerald eyes glinting as she moved. Every step was a calculated glide, her presence as commanding as any queen of the Nile.

She flashed a dazzling smile as she arrived at our circle. Her voice was as silky as the scarf she twirled playfully in one hand. "Don't let Frankie spoil your fun," she teased, her tone light yet carrying an undercurrent of seduction. "There are plenty of us here tonight working to make this evening unforgettable."

Her platinum blonde hair was pulled back into a sleek, low bun, adorned with golden pins that caught the light with every turn of her head. Her makeup was bold, with thick kohl lining her eyes, giving her a look that was both formidable and impossibly chic.

I couldn't help staring at the scarf draped around her neck, a long, gauzy coil fashioned in the likeness of a serpent. I looked more closely. It was hand-painted, with intricate patterns that mimicked scales. The illusion was so convincing it almost seemed alive.

It was mesmerizing. At that moment, I could have sworn the serpent's tongue flicked out—a brief, darting motion so swift and subtle it might have been my imagination playing tricks on me.

"Isn't it divine?" Serena asked, noticing my gaze. With a graceful hand, she adjusted the scarf, and for a fleeting second, the serpent's eyes seemed to blink at me.

"It's stunning," I managed to reply, still unsure if what I had seen was real or merely a trick of the light. Serena's smile widened, as if she relished the unsettling affect her exotic attire had on others.

Serena paused for a moment, her gaze lingering on the empty chair between Violet and Benedict. The professor jumped awkwardly to his feet and offered it to her with a graceful gesture. She eased into the seat with the poise of a queen holding court. Her posture remained impeccably upright, not once leaning back against the chair. Watching her, I sat straighter, mirroring her elegant poise.

Serena turned to Violet, who hadn't yet gotten over Frankie's disrespect. Serena poured salt in the wound.

"Darling, you always manage to look so... ethereal. It's a shame not everyone can appreciate the vintage look day in, day out." Her smile didn't reach her eyes.

She then shifted her gaze toward Sadie with an appraising look. "Sadie, dear, that gown is quite the statement. It almost makes one forget you're more accustomed to dusty tomes than the dazzle of a gala. Almost." Her laugh, light and airy, felt more than a little hollow.

Her attention finally rested on me. "And Marley, isn't that a quaint little gem you're wearing? It has such... charm." She leaned forward to appraise the ruby necklace at my throat. "It's nice to see you're trying to keep up with the rest of us, even if it's only a solitaire."

Her voice dripped with faux sweetness, her eyes glinting with mischief. "Actually, I must commend your simplicity. It's very brave." She gave her head a slight shake and waved an elegant hand in the air. "But then again, I suppose it's best not to compete with the stunning pieces we'll see tonight."

No one gave her the satisfaction of a reply, but Serena didn't mind. After concluding her remarks to the ladies, she shifted her attention to the gentlemen at the table, her demeanor transforming into one of sultry allure.

First, she turned to Jack with a smile that was both inviting and calculating. "Jack, darling," she cooed, her voice a velvety purr as she lightly touched his arm. "It's always a pleasure to see Enchanted Springs' most dashing detective. Tell me, have you solved any heart-wrenching mysteries lately? Or are you saving all your cunning for tonight's performance?" Her laugh was a melodious tinkle, meant to flatter and disarm.

Then, she pivoted gracefully toward Benedict, her eyes softening as she regarded the scholar. "And you must be Professor Cummerbund." He blushed a little, even though she had butchered his name. She took his hand, her fingers lingering a tad too long. "Your brilliance is the talk of the town. I've heard so much about your adventurous research. It must be thrilling to delve into the unknown, to unlock secrets of the past. Surely, tonight's mystery will be child's play for a mind as keen as yours."

Her eyes suddenly darted past Benedict to another figure entering the ballroom. With an excited flurry, she rose from her chair. "Do excuse me," she chimed, her voice lilting with intrigue.

"Alex Trenholm, our man of the hour, has come in. I must have a word with him before he begins the auction."

With that, she rose smoothly from her chair, her golden dress flowing like molten metal, and swiftly made her way toward the newcomer, her serpent scarf trailing behind her with a hiss.

CHAPTER 16

Southern Comfort Gets an Upgrade

MORE SERVERS WEAVED THROUGH the crowd, each bearing trays that carried appetizers so exquisitely presented they nearly halted conversations. Our server approached with a proud flourish. "Smoked Salmon and Caviar Blini," he announced.

Nested in tiny abalone seashells, glittering with opalescent mother of pearl, each smoked salmon and caviar blini was a miniature work of art.

I took one, intrigued. I was able to figure out that "blini" probably referred to the golden pastry at the base, topped with a generous layer of smoked salmon. A dollop of caviar sat atop the salmon, glistening like tiny black pearls.

I could have fit the whole thing in my mouth, but I took a small, delicate nibble, like the fancy grown-up lady I was pretending to be. I was immediately glad I had the sense to savor every bite. The smoky flavor of the salmon perfectly complemented the slight saltiness of the caviar. It was a gustatory glimpse into a world of elegance and sophistication.

Sylvia Robinson swept through the dining room, greeting the guests with her characteristic warmth. Her long, dark hair was styled in a high ponytail, intricately braided and wrapped with a colorful scarf that framed her face. Her strong Georgia accent added to her charm as she stopped by our table, her eyes sparkling with excitement.

When she reached our table, she clapped her hands with joy. "Do my eyes deceive me? If it isn't the charming Miss Marley and the devastatingly handsome detective, Mr. Jack Edgewood!" She laid her hands on Jack's shoulders, rubbing them affectionately. "How you doin', honey?"

Jack's face lit up with pure delight. He beamed at Sylvia, and held up one of her blinis to compliment her.

She laughed. "Quite a step up from my usual shrimp and grits, wouldn't you say?"

He took another bite. "It's amazing, Sylvia. You've outdone yourself."

Sylvia glanced around the elegantly decorated hall with wide-eyed appreciation. "I'd say it's Mr. Lucius Black who has outdone himself. I've never seen an event space look this grand. Whoever that man is, he must have spent a fortune on tonight's setup."

She leaned in closer, lowering her voice as if confiding a secret. "Between you and me, I thought he was a few peaches short of a cobbler when he described what he wanted. All this old-world charm and mystery, like something out of a storybook. But seeing it now, I get it. He turned this old tumble-down hotel into a showplace."

I nodded, my smile hiding the knowledge of the magical underpinnings that made the evening so enchanting. "It's incredible, isn't it? But it's your cooking that puts it over the top."

Sylvia beamed, her eyes twinkling with pride. "I just love feeding folks, doesn't matter if they're dripping in diamonds or barefoot and scrabbling. Food is my way of showin' the love."

She chuckled, her tone infused with pride and a touch of mischief. "Of course, throwin' a little money at the cook never hurt no one."

With a playful shrug, Sylvia continued on her way, still marveling at the surroundings, blissfully unaware of the true depths of the night's enchantment.

The servers returned, weaving smoothly between tables with their trays. In a flawless display of synchronization, they lifted the domed covers to reveal tureens of creamy cauliflower soup.

You might think that sounds pedestrian, especially compared to the aperitifs and appetizers we'd already enjoyed. You'd be wrong.

This soup was like nothing I'd ever tasted. You could serve me this soup every day for the rest of my life and I'd never get tired of it.

I suspect that's because the soup was more cream than cauliflower, blended with garlic and onion and topped with truffle oil.

Violet sighed as she dipped her spoon in and out of her bowl, sipping each bite delicately. I watched, astonished. She almost never interacted with the physical world.

She caught me watching her and grinned.

"Violet, if all you need is a bit of magical moon dust, why don't you enjoy food more often?"

She shrugged, her spoon pausing in mid-air. "It's not that simple."

Benedict dabbed the corner of his mouth with his napkin. "The enchantment here tonight might be the most powerful display of magic I've ever witnessed. I've read about dinners like this, but I think we can assume there's more happening behind the scenes than a sprinkling of fairy dust."

Sadie leaned forward, her eyes reflecting the candlelight. "Exactly. These events, where the paranormal and the physical intertwine so seamlessly, require a depth of magic that's not only powerful but also incredibly delicate. It's like balancing on a tightrope—too much or too little, and the enchantment could completely unravel. And if that happens, you wouldn't want to get caught in the undertow."

As we finished, the battalion of servers whisked the empty bowls from our table. I was admiring their efficiency, watching them work. I barely noticed the slight rustle beside me.

"Pardon me, miss, but did you drop this?" A voice suddenly chimed in next to my ear, pulling me out of my reverie.

CHAPTER 17

Love and Levity

THE SUDDEN MOVEMENT NEARLY made me jump out of my chair. I turned to find a man with a shock of red hair and twinkling blue eyes crouched next to me.

"Sorry to disturb you deary, but I must return your tuppence." He had an Irish brogue and a playful expression.

I blinked, confused. "What?" I was still trying to process his accent.

With a flourish that seemed almost magical, he reached behind my ear and showed me a gleaming gold coin in his outstretched hand. "By gosh and begorah, this must be yours. How else could it get behind your ear?"

I couldn't help but laugh as I finally got the joke. "I don't think that was mine, but thank you," I said, entering into the spirit of his trick.

"My pleasure, darlin'." He stood up straight and handed me the coin with a flourish. "Glen Goldman at your service."

As he rose to his full height, I marveled at his appearance. Along with the shock of curly red hair, he had bushy red eyebrows and a full beard. He was dressed in a jade-green tuxedo that hugged his broad shoulders—but his trousers were just a tad too short. My mother would have called them highwaters, which left his green socks and ankle-high boots on full display.

A voice laced with both amusement and a hint of rebuke called out from behind him. "Glen, dear, are you handing out your hard-earned gold again? I thought we were saving up for the auction tonight."

I turned around. The young woman who approached had a heart-shaped face and long blonde hair, her curls interwoven with garlands of leaves and flowers. Her dress was unlike anything I'd seen before—made entirely of scarves in various shades of green that fluttered with every movement.

Glen's face lit up with a sheepish grin, his earlier confidence melding into tenderness. "Cora, darlin', can't a man show a little generosity?" His tone was light-hearted. but his eyes gleamed with affection when he looked at her.

He grinned widely and reached for her hand, drawing her close. "Cora, my love, I was just making new friends. Allow me to introduce—" He looked at me. "What is your name, sweetheart?"

"Marley," I laughed. "Marley Montgomery."

He nodded as if he was in full agreement. "That's it exactly! Cora, please meet the lovely and talented Marley Montgomery, and all her fine friends." He gestured to me with a flourish.

Cora curtsied. "It's a pleasure to make your acquaintance. But Glen, you know how much I adore that necklace we've come for. I don't know what I'll do if we don't win the auction tonight."

He smiled and took the coin back from me. "'Tis but a jingle of fool's gold, my dear. No fortunes squandered tonight, I promise you. To be sure, any coin I part with this evening will be in the noble pursuit of securing that lovely necklace at the auction for you."

Cora's eyes lit up at the mention of the necklace, her playful suspicion turning into intrigued anticipation. "I should hope so," she smiled. "And I know you are a man of your word."

Glen gave a mock salute. "Every night's a good night for a bit of fun, especially with new friends. Enjoy the dinner, and remember, not all that glitters is gold worth gleaning." With another mischievous grin, Glen and Cora melded back into the crowd, his hand on the small of her back to guide her.

Violet watched as they trailed away. "Don't let the good looks fool you. He's got magic in his veins and mischief in his heart. Did you notice his ears?"

I took another look. He was still close enough for me to see that the tips of his ears were pointed, peeking through the tousled waves of his hair. "Seriously?"

Violet nodded. "If I'm lying, I'm dying."

I put the pieces together, just to be sure. "He's obviously Irish. He's dressed in green, with red hair, pointed ears, and he loves gold. Are you trying to tell me he's a leprechaun?"

Jack nodded. "He's also part Clurichaun, but yes."

"And Cora?"

Sadie took a sip of her drink and set her glass down. "Nymph."

Before I could respond, the chandelier above us swayed slightly, its crystals tinkling like distant bells. My heart skipped a beat, sensing that something was about to happen.

Just as quickly as it started, the lights steadied again, and the sound of subdued conversation slowly resumed.

Jack's eyes met mine, a mixture of concern and determination in his gaze. "Stay sharp, Marley. I have a feeling tonight's only getting started."

I nodded, the uneasy feeling settling deeper in my chest. Whatever was brewing, I knew we were in for a night of surprises—and we hadn't even gotten to the salad course yet.

CHAPTER 18

Salad with a Sidearm

I WAS HONESTLY LOOKING forward to the salads. The menu promised roasted beets and goat cheese, and I knew Sylvia would make it memorable.

No sooner had the salads been served, however, than we were interrupted by the head of security.

"Hey, Jack. I'm sorry to do this, but we've got a situation that requires your expertise." His voice was low but firm.

Jack glanced at me, then back at Eddie. "Sure. Lead the way."

I didn't wait for an invitation; I threw my napkin on the back of my chair and followed.

Eddie took us through the ballroom and into a staff-only area of the hotel. His posture was tense and his pace brisk. We turned down a corridor lined with oil portraits and into a small, dimly lit office.

On the desk lay a dueling pistol, its dark wood and polished metal gleaming ominously under the flickering light.

"This was confiscated from one of the servers," Eddie explained, his tone grave. "We spotted it tucked into his apron."

My breath caught as I took in the weapon's ornate design. We didn't carry firearms at the antique shop, but occasionally people brought them in, hoping to sell.

Unlike the modern firearms I'd seen, this pistol was a work of art. The barrel was long and sleek, made of platinum steel with intricate engravings running along its length. The handle was crafted from polished wood, inlaid with silver filigree.

Jack's eyes narrowed as he examined the weapon. "Who's the server?"

Eddie gestured to the corner, where a young man sat, hands trembling and eyes wide with fear. "He claims he doesn't know anything about it. Says it's not his and he has no idea how it got there."

Jack approached the server, his expression a mix of concern and authority. "What's your name?"

"Ryan," the young man stammered. "Ryan Patrick. I swear, Mr. Edgewood, I've never seen that pistol before in my life. I don't know how it got into my apron. Someone must have put it there to frame me."

Jack glanced back at Eddie, who shrugged. "Given the nature of tonight's event, I thought it best to get a second opinion."

Jack nodded thoughtfully, turning the pistol over in his hands.

"This isn't just any pistol; it's a dueling pistol, period-correct for our 1920s theme tonight. Quite the choice for someone trying to make a statement."

I stepped closer, feeling a chill run down my spine. "Could this be connected to the auction? Maybe someone's planning more than just a bid—perhaps a dramatic recreation gone too far?"

Jack's gaze sharpened as he turned back to Ryan. "Who were you planning to use this on, Ryan? Are you working with someone else here tonight?"

Ryan's eyes widened in panic. "No, sir! I'm telling you, I'm just a waiter. I have no idea how that got into my apron."

Jack sighed, setting the pistol down on the desk. "Eddie, keep an eye on him. We can't afford to take any chances tonight. But let's treat him gently for now—if he's telling the truth, he might be in danger."

Eddie nodded, his expression grim. "Understood."

CHAPTER 19

Night Blooming Jasmine

WE MADE OUR WAY back to the dining room. Sadly, when we returned to the table, my salad plate had been cleared. Sadie was apologetic. "I tried to save it for you, but they were too quick!"

"Maybe Sylvia made extras, and Grandma or Eleanor can grab one for me." When it came to foods I like, I always have a backup plan.

The dinner crowd shifted, a collective pulse quickening as a figure in red glided through the ballroom like a flame cutting through darkness. This must be the jewel collector promised in the evening's program, Jasmine Bloom.

Her beauty commanded every gaze as she approached our table. She had impossibly long legs and implausibly large breasts, with a dress designed to put all of her assets on display. Her hair, black as a raven's wing, fell in lush waves over her shoulders, framing a face that was both hauntingly beautiful and chillingly aloof.

Her eyes, dark and intent, scanned the crowd until they locked onto Violet. Without a moment's hesitation, Jasmine Bloom began making her way toward us, her gaze fixed, her purpose clear.

As she neared, I noticed a delicate pendant nestled against her throat—a black diamond that seemed to absorb light, rather than reflecting it.

Her skin was an unnatural shade of pale, almost translucent under the flickering lights. It gave her an ethereal quality that made her seem as though she was sculpted from moonlight. The skin around her mouth and fingertips bore a subtle hint of blue, suggesting a body accustomed to the cold embrace of the undead rather than the warmth of human life.

Her lips, painted flat, matte black, curved in a knowing smile as she spotted the empty chair directly across from me. With the fluid grace of a cat, Jasmine pulled out the chair, her movements languid yet full of purpose. She perched on the edge of the seat, crossing her legs in a smooth, deliberate motion that caused the slit in her gown to part, revealing a glimpse of her alabaster leg. She sat in a way that claimed more than the chair. She was taking possession of the entire table.

"Good evening," she purred, her voice a velvety whisper that seemed to curl directly into the ears of everyone at the table. "I hope I'm not intruding. It seemed such a waste to see this lovely view unappreciated."

She raised one heavily penciled eyebrow at Violet, and her eyes flickered with disdain. "Or perhaps I'm mistaken. Were you saving this chair?" She laughed, her smile sharp and her fangs bared. This woman was shameless. "Honestly, how long do you plan to keep a seat warm for old flames?" She leaned closer to

Violet, almost menacing. "Old flames—or old ghosts, as the case may be."

Violet returned the woman's cold smile with a forced grin of her own. "Old ghosts have a way of showing up when you least expect them."

Jasmine shrugged, almost imperceptibly. Her laugh, light but with an underlying tension, filled the brief pause that followed. "Old ghosts. Old secrets. They can haunt our daydreams and our nightmares. But tell me, has he ever shown up, even just to say goodbye?"

Violet's cold smile disappeared. "Some things are worth waiting for. Too bad you're not one of them."

Jasmine arched her hand, swiping at the air like a cat. "Meow." Her long fingernails, filed to sharp points and painted black, looked like claws.

For a moment, Jasmine and Violet faced each other, locked in a silent battle of wills. In that moment, Jasmine looked like a woman who existed on the fringes of human vitality, thriving in a realm not entirely bound by the laws of life and death.

Her breathing was shallow, barely perceptible, as if the act of inhaling and exhaling was a forgotten habit rather than a necessity. Her movements were slow, almost languorous, as if she were swimming through the thick air of some opiate dream.

When she finally spoke, her voice was soft yet carried a detached, dreamlike quality, indicative of a mind often caught between the clarity of the present and the shadows of a delirious past.

Her pupils were like pinpoints of midnight in a sea of blue. She blinked slowly, her eyelashes casting long shadows on her pale cheeks, then turned to Jack with a measured grace. Resting her elbow on the table, she slowly traced the blue veins on her arm, from her wrist up to the crook of her elbow, a deliberate motion that highlighted the languid flow of her blood.

"Detective. It's an honor to have you join our little collective this evening."

Jack nodded, his expression neutral. "Miss Bloom."

"Why so formal, my friend? We've known each other for eons." Jasmine's voice had a cutting edge. She leaned slightly closer, her eyes glinting with amusement and challenge. "You know, it does puzzle me why you insist on cloaking yourself in the letter of the law, rather than embracing the freedoms of our kind."

Her smile widened, a hint of mockery dancing in her eyes. "Imagine the good you could do, the justice you could administer, if you weren't so bound by mortal constraints. Join us, Jack. The vampire colony has more to offer than the shadows you're so fond of skulking in."

Jack's response was a tight smile, one that didn't reach his eyes. "Some of us find the light more illuminating, Jasmine. Even if it means standing alone."

Jasmine turned her gaze to Benedict, her eyes narrowing playfully as she shifted in her chair, the fabric of her dress whispering against the polished floor. "And who might you be?" Her voice carried curiosity and a hint of a challenge, as if she already knew more than she let on.

Benedict responded with a reserved but polite smile. "Professor Cumberland." He extended a hand in greeting, and Jasmine accepted it with a flourish.

"Well, Benedict," Jasmine purred, her hand lingering in his for a moment longer than necessary. "I've heard talk of your magical expertise all the way over at the vampire colony. It's not often that someone piques our interest quite like you have."

Benedict's eyebrows rose slightly. "Is that so?"

Jasmine leaned in closer, her voice dropping to a purr that only Benedict and those closest at the table could hear. "Oh, I would never attempt to deceive. But tell me, does your 'job' include charming all those who dwell in the shadows, or am I just fortunate tonight?" Her fingers lightly brushed his arm, the gesture casual yet charged with an underlying intent.

Benedict chuckled, his initial reserve giving way to a more relaxed and engaging demeanor. "I'd say a bit of both. Though I must confess, the charm usually works better on those who aren't already well-versed in enchantment themselves."

Jasmine's smile turned sly, her dark eyes twinkling with amusement. "Ah, but that's where you might be mistaken, Benedict. Sometimes, those who know enchantment best are the ones most susceptible to its effects. It makes the game all the more interesting, don't you think?"

As Jasmine spoke, her presence seemed to cast a subtle spell of its own. It was as if she was both the hunter and the enchantress, weaving her words into a tapestry of intrigue and allure that was difficult to resist. Watching her, I couldn't help but feel that Benedict—despite his own prowess in magic—might find this new "friend" more enchanting and dangerous than he anticipated.

Just as she leaned in closer, a deep, mystical chime resonated through the ballroom, a sound that seemed to come from nowhere yet filled every corner of the room. Jasmine looked up, her expression shifting to anticipation.

"At last," she purred. "The main course." Once again, I caught a glimpse of her fangs, sharp and surprising. "I do hope my steak is served rare."

CHAPTER 20

Dinner Is Served

S UDDENLY, THE CENTER OF the room lit up with a soft, enchanting glow. Above us, ribbons of brilliant green unfurled like celestial banners, weaving through a constellation of shimmering fairy lights. Pink and violet hues fluttered at the edges of the room, as delicate as the petals of a night-blooming flower. The colors shifted and danced, pirouetting in perfect time to the stirring music of the spectral orchestra.

We watched, transfixed, as the lights pulsed across the ceiling, drawing bold strokes of blue and yellow that faded as quickly as they appeared.

Next to me, Sadie gasped in amazement. "It's like a miniature aurora!"

The colors shifted from a deep celestial blue to a vibrant emerald green. Like a liquid rainbow, the flowing array swirled across the ceiling and swayed along the walls, illuminating our faces with visions from a dream.

I was so absorbed by the beauty of it all that I merely gazed in wonder until the celestial show came to an end. As the colored lights faded, we were left staring at a broad expanse of velvet blue, looking for all the world like a quiet starry night.

When I finally looked down, the table had been transformed as well. In front of each of us sat a plate of Beef Wellington, its aroma rich and inviting, with a golden crust that glistened under the soft lighting. Beside it, asparagus draped in hollandaise sauce added a creamy, tantalizing touch to the dish.

"How in the world...?" I turned to Jack.

A knowing smile played on his lips. "Don't tell me," I sighed. "Magic."

I took in the perfectly cooked Beef Wellington and the glossy asparagus. "Well, if this is magic, I'm all for it,"

Around me, others were just as stunned, but the surprise quickly turned into appreciative murmurs as everyone started to dig in. The Wellington was perfectly cooked, the pastry flaky and the meat tender, and the Madeira sauce added richness without being overpowering. The asparagus, sauteed and smothered in a velvety hollandaise, was like a decadent side note to the main melody of the dish.

As we ate, the mood at the table shifted from surprise to contentment. Any tensions from the earlier interruptions began to dissipate, replaced by the soothing ritual of shared food and conversation. I glanced around, taking in the varied expressions of my dining companions.

Sadie was engrossed in her meal, her usual analytical mind momentarily at ease. Violet was chatting animatedly with Benedict, who seemed both amused and intrigued by her ghostly charm.

Jasmine Bloom, however, was another story. She ate with precision, each bite calculated, every movement controlled. Her eyes were anything but calm. They darted around the room, taking in every detail, every whispered conversation, every fleeting expression.

"Enjoying the meal?" I asked more out of politeness than genuine interest.

Her gaze snapped to mine, and for a moment, I saw a flicker of something—impatience? frustration?—before she turned on a charmingly cold smile. "It's exquisite," she replied, her voice smooth as silk. "But then, one wouldn't expect anything less from an evening such as this."

I nodded, not entirely convinced. "You seem preoccupied. Anything we should know about?"

Jasmine's smile widened, but it didn't reach her eyes. "Just thinking about the auction. I am determined to make the Crimson Teardrop my own."

"There's a lot at stake tonight."

She raised an eyebrow, as if she was assessing my meaning, then sipped from her water goblet. "Yes, I suppose there is."

Before I could probe further, a server appeared at Jasmine's side, whispering something in her ear. Her expression darkened briefly, then she composed herself and nodded.

"Excuse me," she said, rising gracefully from her chair. "Duty calls."

Jack leaned over, his voice low. "Keep an eye on her. She's up to something."

I nodded, my curiosity piqued. "You think she's behind the pistol?"

"It's possible," he replied, his tone cautious. "But we can't rule out anyone yet."

We ate in quiet contemplation, the earlier interruption and the mysterious aura of Jasmine Bloom lingering in the back of my mind. As other diners finished their meals, the chatter grew louder, the laughter more genuine, and for a while, it seemed as though the night might pass without further incident.

CHAPTER 21

A Break Between Acts

A S THE DINNER PLATES were cleared away and the guests settled back into their seats, Lucius Black rose to his feet and tapped his glass lightly. The chime of ringing crystal sounded clearly through the air. The conversation hushed and all eyes turned toward him.

"Ladies and gentlemen," he began, his voice smooth and commanding. "Before we proceed to the highlight of our evening—the much-anticipated auction—I invite you all to take a moment to stretch your legs."

A ripple of appreciative murmurs spread through the guests. Lucius's smile broadened, his eyes twinkling with a hint of mischief.

"And, of course," he continued, "I invite you to pass by our lovely and gracious model, Calypso, for one final inspection of the Crimson Teardrop necklace. It's a sight to behold, and I'm sure many of you are eager for a closer look before the bidding begins."

With a gracious nod, Lucius stepped back, and the room began to stir as guests rose from their seats. I stood and stretched, feeling the pleasant weight of the meal settle in my stomach.

"Let's check on Calypso," I said to Jack, who nodded in agreement.

We made our way toward an alcove where Calypso stood, turning this way and that, allowing a throng of guests to admire the necklace. It sparkled brilliantly under the lights, each facet catching the glow and throwing it back in dazzling bursts of color.

Calypso greeted each visitor with a warm smile. As we approached, she stepped toward us.

"Marley, everyone is truly in awe of this necklace. I've been telling them its mystic history, straight from the script."

She touched the necklace lightly with her fingertips and slipped into character. "The Crimson Teardrop is a rare gem, steeped in history and mystery. It's been said to bring great power to its wearer—though, as with all power, it comes with its own set of dangers."

And there it was again: a dark shadow seemed to swirl outward from the ruby, momentarily darkening Calypso's face. In the next instant, it was gone.

I searched her eyes for any sign of distress. "Have you sensed anything strange while you've been wearing the necklace?"

Calypso laughed and shook her head. "Not at all. In fact, it's been a wonderful experience. People are drawn to it, much like moths to a flame. Tonight's auction will be very interesting, I'm sure."

As we stepped away, I couldn't help but scan the room. Jasmine Bloom was circulating among the guests, her presence magnetic. She caught my eye and gave me a cryptic smile before turning back to her conversation.

Eddie stood near the entrance, his gaze sweeping the room. Ryan, the young server, was nowhere to be seen, likely under watchful guard.

"Shall we take our seats?" Jack's voice pulled me back to the present.

I nodded, taking one last look at my necklace, now being celebrated as the Crimson Teardrop. "Let's."

As we returned to our table, the atmosphere buzzed with anticipation. The intermission was drawing to a close, and the auction was about to begin. At that moment, I noticed Jasmine slipping out of a side door, her movements smooth and purposeful.

I decided to follow her. I rose quietly and made my way toward the door Jasmine had used. I moved silently, keeping to the shadows as I followed the faint sound of her footsteps.

Jasmine stopped at a door at the end of the corridor, looking around briefly before entering. I crept closer, peering through the small window in the door. Inside, I could see her talking to someone—a man whose face I couldn't see from where I stood. They seemed to be having a heated discussion.

I strained to hear their conversation, catching snippets of words. "It's now or never... I promise you... No one will know."

My heart pounded, wondering what they were planning. I needed to get closer, to find out what they were saying. I carefully opened the door a crack, slipping inside and hiding behind a large, ornate screen.

"If this doesn't work," the man was saying, his voice low and urgent. "you might not get another chance."

Jasmine sighed. "I'm not sure I have it in me. It seems so final. What if I can't go through with it?"

The man nodded. "Don't worry. Everything is in place. All you have to do is trust me."

Jasmine turned to leave, and I quickly hid around the corner, holding my breath. As t the rohe both left the room, I waited a moment before following, making sure to keep my distance.

Once back in the ballroom, I slipped into my seat as the lights dimmed and a single spotlight illuminated the stage.

CHAPTER 22

Calypso's Song

ALL EYES WERE DRAWN to the light as Calypso stood, silent, unmoving, as ethereal as a marble statue. Her eyes were closed, and her porcelain skin gleamed.

The orchestra played the first notes of a slow, haunting melody began to play. The music was both beautiful and eerie, a song that felt as old as time yet as fresh as the evening breeze.

Calypso opened her eyes and gazed across the room. She raised the microphone and began to sing.

The ruby sun sets,
The day fades away.
I have no regrets.
My love is here to stay.

My heart stopped for a beat as I listened. Calypso's voice was a perfect echo of the record from the shop. The same song, the same longing—it couldn't be a coincidence. The connection was too precise, too poignant.

The audience was spellbound, caught in the siren's enchantment. Even the air seemed to still, and everyone in the audience held their breath as they were swept away by the haunting beauty of her song. Calypso's performance wasn't simply heard; it was felt, resonating in the chest and echoing in the hollows of the heart.

I leaned toward Sadie and whispered. "Hey, Sadie? Do you remember that record from the shop? Could you find anything about the singer?"

She was sipping her drink, and she looked at me over the rim of the glass. "Why are you asking me now? Calypso is trying to sing."

"I know, but this could be important."

She suddenly noticed that her glass was empty, and she frowned. "Oh, man. They're probably not serving drinks during the performance, are they?" She started looking around for a server.

"Never mind your drink. What did you learn about that record?"

Distracted, Sadie glanced at her empty glass and frowned, her attention torn. "Why now, Marley? Can't this wait?"

"No. This might be important."

Her focus returned to me as the last ethereal notes of the song lingered. "I found references, but—"

Benedict hushed her, and she stopped talking. As the last haunting lines of Calypso's ballad lingered in the air, the room remained spellbound, enveloped in the ethereal afterglow of her performance.

Calypso closed her eyes and bowed her head. A collective sigh of release passed through the crowd.

A thunderous applause followed, a testament to the spell she had cast upon every soul in attendance.

Calypso bowed, then bowed again, as the applause filled the room. She stepped to the side, gesturing as the velvet curtains parted gracefully to reveal the stage set behind her.

We were looking at an auctioneer's stand, complete with a polished mahogany podium and velvet ropes. Lucius stepped forward, ready to assume his role as master of ceremonies. Calypso moved to stand beside him.

"Ladies and gentlemen, esteemed guests and creatures of the night, welcome to the highlight of our evening—the auction of the legendary Crimson Jewels.

"Tonight you are part of an exclusive gathering—a privileged assembly. You are guests at an exclusive auction, one where bids are placed not only with currency, but with cunning and courage."

He paused, allowing his gaze to sweep over the crowd, his smile both inviting and mysterious. "The crown jewel of our auction," he continued, gesturing toward Calypso with a practiced flourish, "is the legendary Crimson Teardrop necklace. Beyond its unrivaled beauty, rumors of its mystical powers have enticed collectors from around the globe."

The audience oohed and ahhed in response, the excitement palpable. Lucius smiled broadly. Beside him, Calypso stood as a living testament to its allure. The rubies glinted like drops of blood against her skin, each movement sending flashes of light rippling across the room.

"My friends, this exquisite piece has a history as rich and enchanting as its appearance. Tonight, one of you will have the opportunity to take home this unparalleled treasure."

117

The murmurs in the audience grew, a mix of awe and eager anticipation. Lucius allowed a moment for the fascination to settle before raising his hands for silence.

"Tonight is about more than an auction. It's about desire, about the lengths to which we will go for beauty, and for power." His gaze swept across the room, knowingly lingering on certain guests, hinting at deeper games at play.

"As we lift the veil on 'The Crimson Heist,'" Lucius declared, his voice deepening with intrigue, "remember, everyone plays a part. Trust is a commodity as precious as the jewels we vie for, and tonight, it might be the most elusive treasure of all."

A wave of applause followed his words, the sound swelling and filling the room with renewed energy and anticipation. Lucius waited for the applause to subside before continuing.

"And now, please join me in welcoming our auctioneer for the evening." His voice rose, swelling with the mood of the room. "You know him, you love him! I present to you... Mr. Alexander Trenholm."

CHAPTER 23

The Man, the Myth, the Legend

A LEX TRENHOLM, A DISTINGUISHED fifty-something gentleman with silver hair and a movie-star smile, stepped onto the stage and took his place at the podium after Lucius gracefully exited with a deep bow. Surprisingly, Lucius joined us at our table.

"Thank you, Lucius," Alex said, his voice smooth and commanding as he addressed the sea of eager faces. "Good evening, ladies and gentlemen. It's an honor to be here tonight with Enchanted Springs' most mesmerizing residents."

His bright, keen eyes scanned the audience, his presence magnetic.

"Tonight, we present the Crimson Teardrop, a masterpiece of craftsmanship imbued with ancient powers of protection and prosperity. This piece has graced the collections of royalty and tycoons. It carries tales of fortune and unspeakable tragedy. Its allure is undeniable, but so is its legacy of challenge and change."

He allowed a pause, giving Calypso the chance to turn slowly, showcasing the necklace's hypnotic glimmer.

Alex's tone deepened. "Imagine the power at your fingertips, the envy of your peers," he coaxed. "For centuries, this necklace has been said to possess powers that go beyond mere adornment, protecting its wearer and unlocking the supernatural. But beware, for great power often comes at a great price."

His gaze swept across the audience, his voice rising with the weight of his words. "Who among you will dare to wield such power?"

Calypso stepped forward, allowing the lights to catch the Crimson Teardrop's facets, sending shimmering reflections dancing across the room.

For a moment, I almost forgot I was watching a performance. I was tempted to bid on the necklace myself.

"Who will start the bidding?" Alex called out, his challenge reaching into the heart of every attendee. "Who will claim the magic and the might of the Crimson Teardrop?"

A hush fell over the room, and then the actors began to bid—first one, then another, as they raised their paddles and called out.

Jasmine led with a bid of thirty thousand. Alex swept his hand toward her with a flourish. "Thirty thousand from the radiant Miss Bloom! Do I hear thirty-five?" His voice boomed across the room, resonant and urging, compelling the crowd to push the limits.

From my seat, I watched as the performers raised their numbered placards, each bid punctuated by a theatrical gesture. The atmosphere was charged, almost electric, as the bids climbed higher.

The auction had transformed the room into a theatre of strategy and suspense. As each bid was called, a thrill vibrated through the air, echoing off the grand walls of the ballroom. The spotlight danced from one performer to another, illuminating their faces with a glow that seemed to reflect the fire of the Crimson Teardrop itself.

Cora fluttered her eyelashes at Glen. "Oh, to possess such a gem, to outshine all others," she sighed.

Beside her, Glen nodded enthusiastically. "Consider it yours, my dear. A jewel for a jewel."

The spotlight swung to Glen as he stood. "Thirty-five thousand!" he shouted, holding his placard high. "'Tis small price to pay to bring a sparkle to my lovely lady's eyes."

Frankie raised his placard. "Forty thousand!" He blew a kiss to a random woman seated nearby. "Try to top that!"

For amateur actors, this troop of performers seemed very well prepared. The room was a flurry of silhouettes and shouts as the auction reached its fever pitch. Bids flew, each one higher than the last, a crescendo of voices battling for possession of the coveted Crimson Teardrop necklace.

Jasmine raised her placard. "Forty-five thousand, because true beauty... is priceless."

Lucius chimed in from our table, his tone teasing. "Ah, the stakes are high and so are our spirits! Who can resist such temptation?"

Without missing a beat, Serena stood. "Fifty thousand," she called out, her voice steady and resolute. "For the Crimson Teardrop does not merely adorn; it empowers." Her gaze on the necklace was intense, almost possessive, and I noticed her eyes were glowing green, like the serpent on her scarf.

As the bids soared, Calypso twirled gracefully on her platform, the necklace catching every beam of light, beguiling the bidders and the audience alike.

Glen gave a hearty laugh. "Sixty thousand! Because why bid once when you can bid twice for good luck?"

Alex nodded. "Sixty thousand going once, going twice... Who dares to go higher for the magic within?"

I had to remind myself that the auction wasn't real. It was scripted, well in advance of tonight's performance, but the actors were so convincing that the enthusiasm left us breathless.

Jasmine stood once more, this time her expression somber, her eyes alight with a fierce determination. "One hundred thousand," she stated clearly, her tone commanding the room's attention. "Because some legacies must be preserved, and some powers must be owned to be understood."

Alex nodded approvingly, his gaze sweeping over the audience. "One hundred thousand! Any advance on one hundred thousand?" His voice now held a note of finality, the end of the auction imminent.

A silence fell, heavy and expectant, as everyone seemed to hold their breath. The bidding might have been a game for some, a performance for others, but beneath it all lay currents of desire, ambition, and perhaps even fear.

Frankie, who had been milling about the room, turned toward our table.

"Watch closely now, folks! You wouldn't want to miss the climax of the evening, would you?" As he leaned in slightly, the room suddenly went dark.

There was silence—and then a collective gasp rose from the crowd, a sound made up of equal parts alarm and excitement.

The vibrant energy of moments before turned to confusion and a hint of panic. The sound of uneasy shuffling and hushed voices filled the air.

CHAPTER 24

A Thief in the Night

THE FEW SECONDS OF darkness felt like an eternity. When the lights snapped back on, chaos erupted.

I spotted Calypso standing on the stage, stunned. She staggered backward, one hand clutching her bare neck. The necklace was gone, and blood trickled between her fingers, stark against her pale skin. Her eyes, wide and glassy, seemed to be searching for answers that weren't there.

"Calypso!" I called out, racing to cross the distance between us and join her on stage. Jack and Sadie were quick to follow.

Calypso turned to me, her hands trembling as she clutched the torn fabric of her dress. "Marley, what happened? One moment, I was waiting for the hammer to fall, and then—"

She reached up to feel for the necklace, then gasped. "It's gone!"

She looked at her hand, which was stained with drops of her own blood. "I don't understand." She looked around the floor for the necklace. "Where did it go? Did it fall?"

Her eyes opened wide as the realization hit her. "Marley, that was your necklace."

I gently touched her arm, trying to offer her some comfort. "Let's get you cleaned up," I said, guiding her to a nearby chair. "Sadie, can you get a damp cloth?"

Sadie nodded and raced off, while Jack knelt beside Calypso, examining the wound. "It's not deep, but it looks painful. We should stop the bleeding."

Sadie returned with several clean, folded napkins and a glass of water. Calypso winced as Jack pressed one of the napkins to the wound. "Thank you," she whispered, her voice barely audible over the concerns of the guests.

"What do you remember?" I asked, hoping for some clue. "Anything that might help us figure out who did this?"

Calypso shook her head slowly. "It all happened so fast. One moment, I was standing on the stage, and the next, everything went black. I only remember feeling a sharp pain and then... nothing."

I tried to reassure her. "We'll figure this out. Don't worry. Whoever did this won't get away with it."

"This wasn't in the script." The auctioneer's commanding voice faltered as he stared at us from the podium. Nonetheless, his words carried across the room, and panic began to weave its way through the crowd as reality set in.

The other players gathered near the stage, protesting in confusion.

"This isn't right." Serena shook her head. She was no longer the seductive socialite, charming her way through the audience. She seemed truly stunned. Her carefully cultivated act had dissipated, dissolving into genuine concern.

Glen stood beside Cora, looking frustrated and confused. "We didn't even get to the big reveal." He frowned, and his words hung in the air, adding a layer of surrealism to the already tense atmosphere.

Cora placed a comforting hand on his arm, her face clouded with concern. "That's right," she chimed in, her voice shaking with an undercurrent of anxiety. "Glen was supposed to steal the necklace. It was all planned, down to the last detail."

Glen nodded emphatically, turning to the surrounding crowd as if seeking to affirm the scripted nature of their roles. "It was going to be a grand spectacle," he explained, gesturing with a flair that seemed out of place in the now somber setting. "A bit of fun, a pretend theft. Nothing more."

The audience absorbed his words, but the earlier entertainment now cast in a starkly different light. The high point of the auction had fallen into chaos, leaving everyone to question what they had seen. Was this really happening, or was it still part of the show?

Jack eyed the actors—and the audience—with curiosity and professional courtesy. "Ladies and gentlemen, this is an unexpected turn of events. Please remain seated, and we'll get everything straightened out."

Some people nodded. Others sat down in their chairs in stunned resignation. At that moment, a loud, uncertain voice called out from the back. "Where's Frankie?"

The question seemed to hang in the air, thick with implication.

Suddenly, it all made sense. The conclusion was obvious. Frankie "Fingers" Flynn had never mended his ways. He had taken his role as the evening's rogue to heart, absconding with the Crimson Teardrop necklace under cover of darkness. He had turned a staged theft into a chilling reality. And if Frankie was gone, so was my necklace—possibly for good.

I was about to share my theory with Jack when a piercing scream cut through the chatter. Someone pointed, and there, on the floor beside our table, lay Frankie, a pool of crimson spreading against the white of his shirt.

The shift in the room was immediate. What had been an evening of playful highjinks was now a scene of real horror.

Jack moved quickly toward Frankie, then knelt beside his still form.

I followed. I didn't want to look, but I couldn't miss the fact that Frankie had been hurt. Had he fallen, cutting himself on something I couldn't see? Had he been stabbed? Shot?

I couldn't tell, but the evening's glamour—the opulent decor, the sophisticated guests, the music and laughter—all seemed grotesque and inappropriate now.

Shadows, once playful, now grotesque, danced across Frankie's motionless form, turning this scene of mystical revelry into a tableau of horror.

The enchantment had fractured, revealing its true price, and the sinister undercurrent I had sensed earlier now roared deafeningly in my ears.

It was clear: the bill for our evening of enchantment was steep, and it was ours to settle. The performance had not just gone off script—it had spiraled into nightmare.

CHAPTER 25

An Unqualified Certainty

"**M**ARLEY, DON'T COME ANY closer." Jack's voice was a low command. He stood, his face grim. The others at our table—Sadie, Benedict, and even Violet in her spectral form—looked on in alarm. No one spoke; the playful atmosphere of the murder mystery dinner had shattered completely.

"He's dead," Jack announced, his voice carrying clearly over the sudden silence.

The shock was palpable. Guests began to murmur among themselves. Some rose from their seats, angling for a better view.

I felt a pang of urgency gripping my chest. "But how? Shouldn't we call a doctor?" My voice echoed slightly in the hushed room as I looked from face to face, desperate for some kind of professional assurance. "Is there a doctor in the house?" I was shouting now, hoping against hope.

Jasmine approached, and she and Jack shared a look that carried more weight than words. Their silent communication hinted at deeper, darker truths. They turned toward me, their expressions somber.

"It's too late for a doctor," Jasmine said softly, her tone final. "He's gone."

Panic tightened its grip on me, and I pressed, my voice rising in desperation, "Just like that? What about CPR? What about 911? We should do something!"

Jack guided me to a chair, his face shadowed with the gravity of the moment. "It won't do any good."

I objected further. "You haven't even checked his pulse."

His voice was low but clear enough for those nearby to hear. "I don't need to. People like me, and Jasmine... we can sense when there's no hope of resurrection, no chance of recovery. We can tell when the spark of life, the soul, has slipped away. Frankie's spirit is gone, Marley. And without it, death is an unqualified certainty."

The room fell into a deeper silence following Jack's words, each person grappling with the shock and the abrupt transition from scripted drama to harsh reality.

I looked at Frankie and back at Jack, my voice tinged with urgency. "Should someone call the police?"

Jack's response was immediate. "I am the police, Marley," he reminded me gently. "And more than that, I'm the only paranormal on the police force. Chief Arlington's not a fan of our kind. He didn't hire me by choice. He tolerates me, but only as long as I keep paranormal activities under control and out of the public eye."

The murder mystery dinner had taken a dark, real turn, and now, caught in the middle of it, I was more than a spectator. I was part of the story, whether I liked it or not.

"Why would anyone want to kill Frankie?"

Jack took a deep breath. "That's what I want to know."

He stood taller to face the gathered crowd, all still reeling from the shock, their eyes flicking between him, the body, and the blood-stained stage.

"Ladies and gentlemen," he began, his tone both commanding and reassuring, "I understand this is unusual, but for everyone's safety and to ensure a thorough investigation, I must ask that no one leaves this room until further notice."

As Jack's words hung in the air, a tense silence enveloped the ballroom. The guests began to talk among themselves, the initial shock giving way to a buzz of speculation. Who could have turned a pretend murder into a real one? What was supposed to be a thrilling evening had become a nightmare.

Benedict shuffled over, using his cane to clear a path. "We need to consider everyone here both a witness and a potential suspect until we know more." He looked down at Frankie with a solemn frown.

Eddie Hawkner broke the silence. He had joined us now, and he, too, nodded grimly. "As head of security, I have the authority and the ability to enforce Jack's orders. I think I can speak for both of us that we'll make this as quick and painless as possible."

Lucius Black raised his hand for silence, a signet ring on his fingers catching the light as he did. The room quieted almost immediately, the collective attention shifting toward him.

"Eddie's lockdown is prudent." His voice was smooth and commanding. "Let's not forget the rules of the game we're all playing tonight. The spells that cloak this hotel in magic and mystery hold only until dawn. Once the sun rises, this room, this building, and all its enchantments will dissipate until the next full moon." His gaze swept across the room, ensuring that every participant felt the full weight of his words.

Jack nodded, his face grim with responsibility. "Okay, everyone. You heard the man. We have to solve this here and now, before dawn. Once the sun rises, the enchantment that cloaks this event will lift, and all our suspects, witnesses, everyone, will drift back into the shadows of Enchanted Springs. We can't let that happen—not with a killer among us."

CHAPTER 26

Murder, Unscripted

As Jack finished his warning, I braced myself for panic, for a rush to the exits, for cries of alarm. Instead, a strange, electric current of excitement buzzed through the air. The paranormals around me—creatures of night and magic who had seen centuries, some even millennia—reacted not with fear, but with a gleeful anticipation that prickled my skin.

I glanced around, bewildered. The leprechaun, Glen, clapped his hands with delight and danced a little jig, his eyes twinkling with glee. "Now this is what I call a party!"

Calypso, despite her injuries, laughed aloud—a sound as melodious as it was chilling. "Finally! After decades of make-believe, at last! A true murder mystery! Could there be a more thrilling second act?"

Her excitement rippled through the crowd. Serena smiled broadly, her eyes dancing with delight. "Spectacular," she whispered. "What a stunning turn of events. What a story this will be."

Even Sadie and Violet were swept up in the drama. Violet was floating a few feet above the grown, to get a better view, and Sadie was craning her neck to look around the room. When I caught her eye, she shrugged and shook her head. "Looks like we're not the only ones who find a little danger invigorating," she said.

As for me, I felt like I was standing on the precipice of something monumental. Here I was, surrounded by beings who saw death and disaster as nothing more than an exhilarating challenge. Were they wrong, or were they simply playing the hand life had dealt? After all, how do you fear the end when you've lived through so many beginnings?

What a story this would be—if we lived to tell the tale.

"Indeed," Violet chimed in beside me, her ghostly form shimmering with what seemed like excitement. "And to think, the night is still young!"

As the initial shock of the real murder subsided and the paranormal guests buzzed with excitement and curiosity, Jack's expression hardened with determination. He glanced at his watch.

"Listen up." His voice cut through the crowd, his authority commanding immediate attention. "We're on a tight schedule. The enchantment on this hotel, the magic that keeps this place and its events shielded from the outside world, only lasts until sunrise. That gives us only a few hours to solve this case."

As theories and macabre fascination swirled through the room, Jack's command to stay put had turned the ballroom into a simmering cauldron. Every wayward glance and allegation seemed charged with suspicion and the thrill of the unknown.

"Everyone," Jack's voice resonated with authority as he stepped forward, his detective instincts taking over. "While this may have started as an act, we are now part of a real and serious situation. We need to cooperate and work together to uncover the truth behind this incident."

Beside me, Violet's ethereal form flickered with a spectral glow, her fascination with the night's events clear. "Marley, it seems we've found ourselves in the midst of a genuine mystery—one that not even the spirits could have predicted."

I nodded, my mind racing. The blend of paranormal entities in the room, each with their own centuries of secrets and sagas, added layers of complexity to the situation. "Violet, do you think any of the other guests knew what was going to happen tonight?"

She floated closer, her voice a ghostly whisper. "In a room full of immortals and mystics, dear, secrets are both currency and weapon. Watch closely. Notice who reacts and how. The guilty often reveal themselves not by their actions, but by their reactions."

As the crowd's initial shock morphed into a mix of intrigue and analytical observation, I scanned the room. Serena, her earlier gaiety subdued, now looked pensive, her gaze darting around as if piecing together a puzzle. Glen, still maintaining his mischievous cheer, seemed more observant than his carefree demeanor suggested.

Suddenly, the kitchen doors swung open. Grandma Clara came out first. She looked around the ballroom with a curious expression and a practiced calm. She made her way through the crowd with a grace that belied her years, stopped when she saw the body, and wrapped her arm around me in a firm, reassuring embrace.

Eleanor followed close behind. Her hands wrong the hem of her apron and her eyes darted around the room as she took in the unusual scene. "Oh, my stars. What on earth has happened here?"

Bringing up the rear was Sylvia, the caterer. Her eyes were open wide and she shook her head in disbelief, completely baffled by the scene unfolding in the room. Unlike the seasoned paranormals reveling in the night's drama, Sylvia was unmistakably out of her element, a mere mortal caught in a whirlwind of supernatural intrigue.

My grandmother took Sylvia by the arm, her voice low but clear. "Don't worry, dear," she soothed, patting Sylvia's hand gently. "It's all part of the murder mystery game."

Grandma Clara reached into the pocket of her apron and discreetly pulled out a small vial containing a shimmering dust. With a practiced hand, she sprinkled a pinch of the luminescent powder over Sylvia and whispered a soft incantation under her breath. Her movements were almost imperceptible.

"The party planners have done a remarkable job," Gram continued, her tone light and reassuring. Sylvia nodded, her expression relaxing as the pixie dust subtly altered her perception, smoothing over the edges of her alarm. Her eyes lost their edge of panic, replaced by a serene acceptance. "Oh, I see," she said, a gentle smile curving her lips. "It's all so... theatrical."

"Yes, indeed," Clara agreed, giving Sylvia a comforting squeeze on the shoulder. "Now, your work for the evening is done. Why don't you go back to the kitchen and take a little break? Get yourself a glass of water and put your feet up for a moment. We'll be in soon to get the desserts ready. Trust me, they're heavenly."

With a renewed calm, Sylvia turned back toward the kitchen, her previous anxiety replaced by a tranquil composure. She was ready to continue her role as caterer, blissfully unaware of the deeper magical currents flowing through the night.

I stopped her as she passed by me.

"Sylvia?"

She looked at me with sparkling eyes, a gentle smile spread softly across her face.

"Yes, Marley?"

"If you have any of that salad left, could you fix me a container to go? I didn't get a chance to finish mine."

She reached out to stroke my arm affectionately. "Oh, you poor thing! Yes, child. I'll make sure you get a heaping helping to take home."

CHAPTER 27

Through the Lens of Time

G RANDMA CLARA TURNED TOWARD Jack. "Detective, could you please explain what's going on here? Why is Francis Flynn lying dead on the floor?"

Jack nodded thoughtfully. "I'm working on it, Clara. It's an active investigation."

Gram looked at me. "What happened, Marley? Why do I get the sense that you're part of this?"

I exchanged a glance with Sadie, gathering my thoughts before diving into the night's bewildering events.

"It started with the necklace I found back at the shop," I began, the image of the stunning piece vivid in my mind. "It was supposed to be a prop for tonight's game."

Sadie nodded in agreement, taking over the narrative. "Calypso borrowed Sadie's necklace to wear for the auction. It was all part of the script... until it wasn't." Her voice faltered slightly, the shock of the evening still fresh. "Just as the auction was coming to an end, someone ripped it from her neck."

We looked over at Calypso and Lucius, now standing near a portable bar. The high-end fixture looked like a smaller version of the bar in the speakeasy, constructed from rich walnut and polished to a high sheen. The top was a seamless slab of polished onyx, and the front was adorned with art-deco inlays.

Calypso had regained her composure, and her poise and elegance had returned. For a moment, everything about her seemed perfectly normal. But then, her smile faltered, and her eyes briefly clouded with what looked like confusion or pain. She touched her bodice subtly, her fingers brushing against the fabric as if to quiet her heart. The moment passed quickly and Calypso closed her eyes and sighed.

I turned to Eleanor, who furrowed her brow in concern. "Which necklace are we talking about?" Her voice carried an urgency that hinted at deeper layers of worry.

Without missing a beat, Sadie pulled out her phone and quickly scrolled through the photos. She stopped on the selfie she had taken earlier with Violet and me. It showed the three of us, smiling for the camera in our vintage dresses.

Sadie handed the phone to Eleanor, who took it, her eyes narrowing as she examined the image. Her face faltered as her eyes zeroed in on my necklace.

"Oh, my," Eleanor gasped, her hand flying to her mouth. "Marley, where did you find that necklace? Oh dear, this is most unfortunate."

Clara leaned over to view the screen, her sharp gaze taking in every detail. "This was no ordinary necklace, was it?"

I nodded, feeling a pang of guilt. "I thought it was costume jewelry."

Eleanor looked at the photo again, her fingers brushing the screen as if she could feel the gems through the glass. "I remember that necklace. It was always meant to be kept safe, guarded. But for the life of me, I can't recall where it came from or why it needed such protection."

Clara looked at me. "That's not the necklace you're wearing it now."

I reached up to touch the ruby solitaire Calypso had given me earlier in our exchange. "No. I let Calypso borrow my necklace for her act."

Eleanor's brow furrowed, her memories seemingly sifting through the fog of time. "That necklace... it's not just any piece of jewelry. It was meant to be locked away."

Clara looked at her friend with concern. "Eleanor, what do you mean?"

The older woman shook her head, her hands trembling slightly as she tried to grasp at elusive threads of her past experiences. "There was something about that necklace—a history, a curse, or was it a haunting? I'm not sure, but I do know it was supposed to be hidden away."

Sadie leaned in, her curiosity overtaking her initial shock. "You mean it's an artifact? With real historical and magical significance?"

"Yes, exactly," Eleanor nodded, her brow furrowed in frustration at her fading memories. "It was an important piece. Oh, I thought I had done enough by keeping it secure in the storeroom, but it seems I was mistaken."

Jack, who had been listening, stepped closer, his interest piqued. "Eleanor, anything you can recall might help us figure out what happened tonight."

Eleanor sighed, her gaze distant. "Let me think. It's all a bit muddled. But I do remember there was a reason we kept it secured. Oh, if only my mind were as sharp as it used to be!"

As she spoke, it seemed like the glittering chandeliers were casting long shadows, and my breathing grew shallow as I tried to come to terms with my role in the drama.

Eleanor looked around nervously, her eyes flitting between the reveling guests and us. "I'm sorry. I can't remember the details." Her voice was strained. "I'm sure it will come to me, but my memory isn't what it used to be."

She looked at me sadly. "Time travel, my dear. It takes more than moments. Sometimes, it takes your memories too."

My grandmother wrapped her arms around Eleanor's shoulders. "Don't worry, dear. Jack will get that necklace back."

She sighed, a deep, weary sound. "I hope so. All I know is that the necklace was part of something bigger, something important."

Benedict, who had been quietly observing, chimed in smoothly. He seemed to be slipping into his professorial mode.

"This reminds me of the Hope Diamond. Originally stolen from a Hindu statue, believed to curse its owners from French kings to other nobility. Most famously, it was owned by Louis XVI and Marie Antoinette before their executions. Now, it's merely a tourist attraction in the Smithsonian, but its legend of misfortune lives on." His suggestion hung in the air, both an offering and a veiled prompt.

Sadie's eyes lit up with recognition, the scholar in her sparked, too. "Yes, and it's fascinating how often artifacts are imbued with legend and lore. It's hard to say whether those tales stem from actual magical properties or the human penchant for storytelling."

She leaned closer, her gaze intent as she studied the photo again on her phone. "Marley, this could be a significant piece, historically and magically. If we're going to recover it, we might need to dig deeper into its past."

I remembered back to the auctioneer. "Maybe it's cursed, like the auctioneer said."

Sadie shook her head. "Technically, he was reading from a script. That was simply part of the performance, designed to add a layer of intrigue to the murder mystery dinner."

"But there could be an element of truth in the auctioneer's story."

"It's possible. But how do we separate fact from fiction?"

I mused aloud, remembering back to all the old paperwork I'd sorted on my desk. "Maybe there's something in the files back at the shop."

I turned to my mentor, hoping for a lead. "Eleanor, do you think there are any notes in our files? Did you keep any records that might help?"

"There could be something," Eleanor replied, her voice tinged with caution. "But be careful, Marley. Secrets are usually hidden for good reasons." Her words, heavy with unspoken history and warnings, made me pause.

Grandma Clara nodded slowly, her voice steady despite the rising chaos around us. "Then it sounds like we need to find out exactly what that 'something' is, and quickly. Before this night unravels any further."

Her words hung between us, heavy with unspoken history. I felt a resolve settling in me, a determination to restore order and uncover the truth. I knew I would do whatever it took to get the necklace back from the thief.

The hum of the crowd filled the air, mingling with the soft clinking of glass and the distant strains of music that had resumed at a lower volume. The task felt daunting, but I knew I would do whatever it took to retrieve the necklace and unravel the mysteries it held.

"Don't worry, Eleanor." I nodded my head, partly to reassure myself. "I'll find out. We'll get to the bottom of this."

CHAPTER 28

Time Stands Still

THERE WAS JUST ONE problem: we were on lockdown. I knew there was no way I could sneak past Jack, Lucius, or Eddie, the head of security.

I turned to Sadie, feeling a sense of urgency, knowing that the clock was ticking. "Sadie, we can't just stand here. We need to act."

Her expression wavered between worry and resolve. "There is something we could try, but it's a bit... unconventional."

I smiled. "Since when do we play by the rules?"

Sadie exchanged a look with Benedict, who gave a subtle nod, the seriousness in his eyes mirroring the gravity of our situation.

Sadie took a deep breath. "We could freeze time." Her words hung heavy in the air. "Just long enough to get some answers without interference."

I shrugged. "Okay. I'm in. Let's do it."

Sadie shook her head slowly. "It's not that easy." She turned to Eleanor and Clara. "Are you familiar with the Temporal Stasis spell?"

Eleanor perked up. "Of course!" She leaned forward, worry lining her face. "But that's an advanced manipulation of time. It requires a trio of talented, natural-born spellcasters to perform it properly!"

I felt overwhelmed. "I don't know the first thing about casting spells like that," I admitted. I'd only come into my magic a few months earlier.

Clara chimed in, her eyes twinkling. "Well, we've got Eleanor and Sadie. And as a temporal witch, I can certainly lend my energy, as well."

A sly grin spread across Benedict's face. "At the risk of sounding immodest, I happen to be a Level Six Spellcaster. Working together, we could indeed freeze time within the boundaries of Enchanted Springs. Just long enough for you to investigate, Marley."

Sadie nodded slowly, mulling it over. "It's risky, and not exactly by the book, but these are extraordinary circumstances. With careful control, we might manage it without disrupting too much of the temporal balance."

I looked from my grandmother to Eleanor, who were glancing warily around the room. "You two seem unconvinced. Is it dangerous?"

They nodded, and Benedict answered. "Extremely," he confirmed, his voice steady. "But warranted, given what's at stake."

With a resolve that surprised me, I nodded. I was determined to proceed, no matter the risk. "Do it. I'll go back to the shop and learn what I can, as quickly as I can. There's got to be a clue about the necklace somewhere."

Eleanor reached out, touching my arm gently. "You might need to journey farther than you expect. Be careful, Marley. Delving into the past can be as dangerous as ignoring it."

My grandmother took my hands in hers. Her eyes were kind, but her expression was serious. "Remember, Marley, every action in the past could ripple into unforeseen consequences. Go, but tread carefully."

Sadie clasped her hands together, looking from face to face. "All right. It's settled. Let's prepare the spell. This could be our only chance to get to the bottom of this mystery before dawn breaks and the enchantment on the hotel lifts."

Gram reached into her apron pocket and handed me the keys to her bakery van. "I parked out back, near the service entrance."

The four of them formed a circle around me and linked arms, forming a chain of concentrated power. I looked over toward Jack: luckily, he was deep in conversation with Eddie, and his back was turned.

My friends' voices joined in a soft incantation, a slow and measured chant in perfect syncopation, like the ticking of a clock.

The air around us shimmered with a subtle luminescence, the threads of magic visible like fine silk caught in sunlight.

In the ballroom, the crowd stilled, and an otherworldly hush descended. The vibrant laughter and clinking of glasses came to a standstill, as if the very essence of time itself had been ensnared by our spell. Guests mid-gesture were suspended in a tableau of frozen revelry; a waiter stood poised with a tray of sparkling champagne, his foot raised in midair. A woman was caught in the act of adjusting her gown, one hand pulling at her bodice. The delicate flutter of a dropped napkin hung motionless in the air, its descent toward the polished floor paused in defiance of gravity.

The grand chandeliers above ceased their soft swaying and the gentle flicker of candlelight stilled, casting unwavering beams that spotlighted the faces of the motionless crowd. Their expressions were preserved in perfect stillness—smiles etched on their lips, and eyes wide with laughter or intrigue. The space outside our circle seemed as still and quiet as a painting.

With a nod from Eleanor, I ducked beneath their linked arms and stepped out of the circle. The contrast was startling. As I moved, the rustle of my dress and the soft tap of my shoes on the marble floor seemed unnaturally loud in the silent, frozen world.

I didn't linger to marvel at the eerie beauty of the ballroom suspended in time. Instead, I hurried toward the exit, each step echoing in the vast, motionless space, a lone figure moving through a world paused indefinitely.

I passed stragglers in the lobby, the doorman at his post, a uniformed chauffeur in the parking lot, one hand raised to light a cigarette as he leaned against the trunk of his car. All were silent and unmoving.

I ran toward my grandmother's van, and the night held its breath as I headed off to uncover truths hidden by time and magic.

CHAPTER 29

Portal to the Past

A S I DROVE THE van through the empty streets of Enchanted Springs, the silence of the night was as thick as fog. The full moon cast long shadows, turning familiar intersections into a ghostly maze. Each stoplight, unlit and useless, reminded me how alone I was out here. The van's engine hummed a steady rhythm, the only sound in the eerie quiet, as if reinforcing that I was on the right path. I wasn't simply headed to the shop. I was steering a course for understanding. Now that I had stepped into my birthright as a time-traveling witch, this wasn't merely my role. It was my responsibility

Gripping the steering wheel, I could feel the weight of everything that had happened, pressing down like the darkness around me. The shop, with all its mysteries and memories, felt like a test. What would I find there? What was I even looking for? The questions haunted me, swirling in my mind like the leaves that danced across the moonlit road.

This wasn't just a drive; it was a journey into the unknown parts of myself. With each passing block, I felt the pull of my family's legacy and the heavy responsibility of the powers I had inherited. The night wasn't simply a shield from the eyes of the town; it was a mirror, reflecting back the parts of myself I was still learning to face.

The shop was eerily silent as I stepped inside. The familiar tinkle of the bell above the door sounded louder in the stillness of the night.

My heart raced as I moved purposefully toward the back of the store. There, on my desk, was the that had once cradled the now-missing necklace.

I picked it up and turned it over. The leather exterior was dusty, but unmarked. I opened the hinged lid and saw a gold stamp inside the cover, faded but still legible. I turned on my desk lamp to see it better.

"Crafted by DeLuna Jewelers," it read. The old-fashioned script hearkened back to a bygone era of elegance and sophistication.

I traced my finger over the embossed lettering, feeling the texture under my fingertips. DeLuna. The name wasn't familiar, but then again, my knowledge of local businesses from a century ago was admittedly sketchy.

I pulled out my phone to do a quick search. I found a brief mention in a digital archive of the Enchanted Springs historical society. As it turns out, DeLuna Jewelers had been a fixture in downtown Enchanted Springs for fifty years—but the shop had closed in 1940.

I recognized its location: the old Enchanted Springs Emporium. That was a former department store that now housed the Enchanted Springs Art Museum.

I took a deep breath. I could go there, back in time. If I could see the jewelry shop in person, maybe I could figure out why the necklace was so important.

My footsteps echoed the soft ticking of the old grandfather clock as I made my way to the storeroom. The cluttered space looked like any other storage room in a vintage business. No one who happened to peek inside would ever guess that it housed a cosmic portal. It was the least conspicuous place imaginable for a a doorway through time.

The shop's logbook lay open beside me on a cluttered shelf, its pages filled with notes and dates of previous journeys. I flipped through the entries, searching for a date that hadn't been visited by anyone from the future.

Ah, here was one: a summer's day in mid June, 1925. That would put me in the heart of the Roaring Twenties, and no one from the shop had traveled there before. It was the perfect setting to uncover the secrets of DeLuna Jewelers.

With a deep breath, I focused on the date I'd chosen, my hand lingering on the last entry in the logbook.

I felt the air begin to hum, like a coil in a Faraday cage. The floor seemed to fall away beneath my feet, and I was engulfed in a whirl of spinning lights and vibrant colors. The familiar surroundings of the storeroom blurred as the present melted away to reveal the past. I felt like a feather caught in a windstorm, pulled and pushed from all directions.

Instinctively, I held my breath and shut my eyes tight, bracing myself against the cosmic flow of time and space. Then, as quickly as it had begun, the motion stopped, the world steadied, and I opened my eyes to find myself in the same place, but in a vastly different time.

CHAPTER 30

June 17, 1925

I COULD TELL THE journey had been successful. Gone was the clutter of the antique shop, with dusty shelves of vintage merchandise. Instead, the storeroom was meticulously organized, reflecting a bygone era's need for order and efficiency.

In this time, the antique shop had been a mercantile, an all-purpose general store that catered to everyday needs during the Coolidge years. The old wooden shelves were neatly labeled with hand-painted signs: tools, textiles, dry goods. Large bins of dried beans and rice sat alongside barrels of salted meat, all essential for the mercantile's day-to-day operations.

The air was filled with the scent of fresh cedar and linseed oil, a sharp contrast to the musty, forgotten corners of my time. The floor, previously a maze of scattered heavy items, was now a clean expanse of polished wood. In the corner, where a pile of broken furniture once languished, stood a craftsman's workbench, complete with an array of well-maintained tools, each hanging in its designated spot.

When I stepped out of the storeroom and headed to the front of the shop, I was surprised by the bright daylight streaming through the windows. Of course. I'd chosen to arrive in the middle of the day, not the middle of the night.

The store's layout was essentially unchanged, lending a familiar feel to the space. Instead of vintage collectibles, I saw spools of thread, bolts of calico fabric, and buttons neatly tacked onto printed cardstock. Cotton sacks of flour were stacked beside shiny tins of coffee and jars of local honey. Nothing fancy. Just the essentials, all under the watchful eye of Peter Johnston, the 1925 proprietor.

I first met Peter during my orientation, when Eleanor and my grandmother Clara introduced us. In the store's entire history, there had only been four principal shopkeepers: Martha Snow, Peter Johnston, Eleanor, and me.

As I made my way to greet him, a familiar, flickering figure caught my eye. Twila, the same spectral Siamese kitten who frequented the premises in my time, was curled in a beam of sunlight. She opened one sapphire eye, regarded me with curiosity and indolence, then yawned and drifted back into her sunlit dreams.

Peter was behind the counter. A slight smile creased his face when he looked up from his ledger and saw me approach.

Peter looked like he was in his late fifties or early sixties. He was mostly bald, and the hair that remained was white with age and combed straight back. He wore a simple canvas apron over a button-up shirt, complete with rolled-up sleeves, and he peered at me over wire-rimmed glasses perched on the end of his nose.

154

"Hi, Mr. Johnston." I nodded toward the sunlit corner where Twila lay, her form flickering slightly in the dappled light. "I see your assistant is hard at work."

Peter chuckled softly, his eyes following mine. "Ah, that little sprite flits in and out like a breeze through an open window. Always on her own terms, that one."

"She's the same in our time." I think she knew we were talking about her, but she merely yawned and stretched languidly in the sun.

"Really? I hadn't realized." Peter shook his head, a hint of astonishment in his tone. "Not surprising, though, now that I think of it. She's been here as long as I can remember. She looks like an ordinary kitten, but..."

I nodded. "She does come and go on her own schedule, doesn't she?"

Peter sighed. "If you didn't know any better, you'd swear that little kitten is the true owner of the shop."

Peter's eyes were bright and clear, and he didn't miss a thing. He looked me up and down, a slight smirk playing at the corners of his mouth.

"What brings you to this sunny corner of history?" His voice carried the distinctive twang of old Florida.

I hesitated for a moment before showing him the empty jewelry box. I knew my story was a lot to unpack, but here in the past, I had plenty of time.

I briefed him on the murder mystery dinner, the turmoil among the paranormals, and my quest to uncover the truth behind the necklace at the center of it all.

Peter listened intently, his eyes sharp and understanding. His ability to follow my story was a testament to his grasp of the tangled threads of fate and magic, despite the fact that he was rooted in the early twentieth century.

"Did your grandmother and Eleanor sanction this little time jaunt?" Peter asked, his tone both stern and concerned.

"Yes, sir. They did. They even froze time to give me a chance to make this trip, with something called the 'Temporal Stasis Spell.'"

Peter nodded slowly. He reached for the necklace box, which I had set down on the checkout counter. His eyes twinkled with mischief, yet there was a note of caution in her tone as he took the box and tucked it under the counter.

"Well, if you're headed over to the Emporium, it's best we keep this artifact from the future safe right here. We don't want any crosscurrents ripping holes in our universe, now do we?"

He chuckled softly, then turned to open the old brass cash register that had been ringing sales in the shop since 1910. I still used it myself, back in the future. As the cash drawer opened, the familiar chime was oddly comforting.

He lifted a secret compartment in the bottom of the cash drawer, then carefully laid several gold certificates on the counter. They looked like hundred-dollar bills, but each one was marked with its value in gold. "These should cover your needs," Peter continued, pushing the certificates toward me. "They're as good as gold, literally."

I counted them out. It was far more money than I'd expected. I looked at him in surprise.

"This is eight hundred dollars! It's a lot of money in my time. It must be a fortune in yours."

He nodded. "Yep. But you'll need it if you want to be a customer of Daniel LaLuna."

I couldn't have accepted such a large sum if I hadn't been privy to some insider information: the Council of Guardians who set up the Enchanted Antique Shop also ensured a generous cash reserve, based on a long-range view of the stock market and the global economy. You could almost say it was a form of insider trading, but since it was for the benefit of history—and humanity—I knew we could afford it.

Even so, I held up my hand to stop him. "I wasn't planning to buy the necklace. We're not supposed to take artifacts back that would be missed in their own time."

Peter's eyes twinkled with mischief and wisdom as she handed me the money. "Sometimes, the course of history requires a nudge to align things just so. If you find that necklace is indeed as central to the troubles in your time as you believe, purchasing it could be that nudge. Think of it not as removing something, but as relocating it for its own protection—and yours."

Peter leaned in, his expression serious yet lined with an understanding of the extraordinary. "And remember, if that that necklace is enchanted, it isn't bound by our notions of time and place. It could be a creation that transcends the ordinary, capable of causing chaos across the ages. If it's stirring up trouble in your time, it was likely never meant to settle into the flow of history quietly. Your intervention might well be part of your destiny."

He paused, a thoughtful frown creasing her brow. "Some magical artifacts chart their own courses, wandering through time as they see fit. Securing it might stabilize things more than you realize."

"Should I take off the one I'm wearing now?" I asked, touching my borrowed necklace.

"Wouldn't hurt. Best not to mix your currents more than you've already done."

I handed it to him and he tucked it into the empty necklace box, then winked as he gestured toward the door. "Off you go, Miss Montgomery. See you soon."

CHAPTER 31

An Unexpected Encounter

WITH THE GOLD CERTIFICATES tucked into a borrowed clutch, I stepped out onto the bustling Main Street of Enchanted Springs, 1925.

The first thing that hit me was the noise. My hometown of old was buzzing like a beehive, and the street was packed with people—women linked arms and chatted as they strolled, stopping to gaze at store window displays. Men in sharp suits tipped their hats, dogs and children ran along the sidewalk, and horses and cars shared the road in a chaotic dance. The air was filled with the sounds of hooves, the clatter of carriage wheels, and the occasional honk of early automobiles.

The past was alive, and I was walking right through it.

I glanced down at my cocktail dress, feeling a wave of relief that at least I looked the part of a genuine 1920s citizen.

Then I saw her, and I wondered why she had followed me back through the portal.

"Violet," I called. I took a few steps forward, waving to catch her attention. "Violet! Hello!"

At the sound of her name, she turned toward me. She looked just as surprised to see me as I was to see her. She was dressed in a smart, knee-length day dress adorned with subtle embroidery, along with a cloche hat that hugged her neatly styled bob.

I scurried to meet her where she had stopped. I was a little out of breath. "Hey, Violet. I didn't see you come in when I was back in the shop. What are you doing here?"

She looked me over, her gaze sharp and calculating. She studied my face curiously, snapping her gum, a flicker of confusion in her eyes. "Look, kitten, you seem like a real sweet doll, but I don't know you from Adam. How do you know my name?"

I realized with a start that I was face to face with Violet before she... transitioned. Of course she didn't know me. We wouldn't actually meet in person for more than a hundred years. Come to think of it, I wouldn't be born for another seventy years.

"Something tells me we don't run in the same circles." Her eyes narrowed slightly as she took in my formal gown. Her voice was tinged with amusement. "You're all dolled up like you're headed off to a soirée at the Ritz."

She blew a bubble with her gum while she waited for my response. I looked down at my long dress and shrugged. "Well, I'm going somewhere later. I won't have time to change."

She grinned good-naturedly. "That's really swell, toots. You're gonna knock 'em dead. But all I know is I've gotta hop, quick like a bunny. My husband's waiting, and he's got the car running."

A tilt of her head suggested she found my overdressed appearance a curious anomaly rather than a social faux pas. "You're a gas, and as much as I'd like to chew the fat, I gotta fly. Duty calls, and my fella's not the patient type."

With that, Violet winked conspiratorially, as if we shared a secret joke, and then she was off, the heels of her strappy shoes clicking briskly on the pavement as she merged back into the crowd. She didn't turn to face me again, but she raised her arm in a playful wave and walked away.

CHAPTER 32

The Enchanted Emporium

I TOOK A DEEP breath to refocus. The museum—or rather, the Emporium—was just up the street, so I carried on with my mission.

As I reached the old department store, I marveled at the difference between the building in my time and now, back in the past. Here in 1925, the Enchanted Springs Emporium was in its heyday. The cream-colored brickwork was fresh and clean, trimmed with vibrant green and burgundy bands around arched windows and Roman columns. The colors were inviting, enticing, drawing shoppers in from up and down the street. It looked grander, somehow, than it did in my time.

Stepping inside was like walking into another world. In the twenty-first century, the museum was quiet and hushed. During the day, it was never crowded. Occasionally, a few new patrons ambled through, thoughtfully perusing the exhibits. As a museum, the only sounds were the quiet conversations of art lovers and the occasional guided tour.

In this time, however, the grand old building was bustling. Shoppers hurried from counter to counter, asking to see scarves and hats. The young women working as clerks juggled boxes and tissue paper so customers could see the merchandise. Everyone was chatting and laughing, sharing small talk and snippets of gossip. It felt strange to see the building so alive.

The hardwood floors gleamed underfoot, obviously well cared for. I could smell floor wax and perfume, scented talc, and the occasional whiff of someone who'd been out in the sun. The store was air conditioned, and ceiling fans rotated overhead, but Florida is Florida, and there's no avoiding the heat of the day. Oddly enough, I also noticed the distinctive scent of Chanel N°5. To me, it was a timeless classic, but in 1925 it was a new perfume. As I passed a cosmetic counter, a salesgirl offered free samples. I reached out my arm and she misted my wrist.

I spotted the jewelry shop in the far corner. I was surprised by the way it sat apart from the rest of the store. Back in my time, it was simply one corner of the overall museum space. Here in the Emporium, however, the quiet nook had been transformed into an enclave of elegance and charm. Half walls of paneled mahogany rose up from the marble floor. Arched windows of lead glass beckoned, inviting shoppers to peer in wonder at a tantalizing display of precious jewels.

I stepped through a doorway flanked by intricately carved oak columns, as if I was stepping into another world.

Inside, the space unfolded like a treasure chest. Glass cases lined the room, sparkling with an array of brooches, rings, and hat pins, each placed to catch the light and gleam enticingly. An array of necklaces and bracelets, each carefully arranged on plush velvet stands, gleamed in the sunlight.

A jeweler stood from a workbench to greet me. He was probably in his forties, with a hint of silver in his otherwise dark hair. It was parted neatly to one side, Clark Gable style, and his eyes were warm and welcoming.

He smiled as I approached. "Can I assist you, miss?" His tone was both curious and cautious. Maybe my evening gown was throwing him off.

"I'm looking for a very specific piece," I began, my voice steady despite the surreal nature of my visit. I described the necklace in as much detail as I could remember. "It has pearls, and clear crystals, and an oversized ruby teardrop as its centerpiece."

He paused, his expression turning thoughtful. "Ah, you mean the Sunset Ruby." His voice tinged with pride as he reached into a glass display case.

He pulled out a stunning necklace, its central gem catching the light with a fiery glow.

"That's it!" I exclaimed, unable to hide my surprise.

He laid the necklace on a velvet cushion, allowing me to admire its craftsmanship. "I created this piece after seeing a mesmerizing singer perform at a local venue. Her voice was as captivating as the sunset itself. But she was like a comet—brilliant but fleeting. After she finished her set, I never saw her again."

He sighed. "Arabella Delarosa was the brightest star of the Lydia Lounge. I crafted the Sunset Ruby necklace for her, hoping to capture even a fraction of her radiance. But after that night, she seemed to vanish from the face of the earth."

The surrealism of the moment wasn't lost on me; I was looking at a necklace in 1925 that I knew had magical powers. I knew it would be hidden, then found. I knew that it could change the future—because it had already changed the past, leading me here, to a jeweler back in time.

I looked from the necklace, back to the jeweler. "The ruby is beautiful. Where did it come from?"

He reached for the necklace, lifting it toward the light. He had long fingers, like an artist or a musician. "Oddly enough, the stone was a gift. It came from Theodore Stevens' estate. After his death, his widow no longer wanted to own it—or to sell it. Her maid brought it in and insisted that I keep it."

Interesting. Maybe it truly was cursed.

My mind was racing. If I bought it, would I change the future? If I slipped it out of this timeline and into my own, would it be less dangerous—or more? I wondered about the ripples I was sending through time. Would history be changed, or would time simply flow inevitably to the same destination?

"Do you like it?" the clerk asked, his voice pulling me back from the brink of an existential spiral.

"It's beautiful."

I reached out, my fingers hovering over the necklace. The temptation to take it back to the Enchanted Antique Shop was overwhelming—but the risks were daunting.

"Would you like to try it on?"

I nodded, almost mechanically. As he clasped the necklace around my neck, I felt a chill. Not from the pearls against my skin, but from the realization that I was now part of its history. A part that no one, not even the spirits at the antique shop, could have foreseen.

"It suits you," he said, holding a hand mirror for me to look into. "The pearls compliment your skin tone, and the ruby casts a certain glow across your complexion."

I stared at my reflection, at the necklace that seemed both new and impossibly old.

"I'll take it," I said, my decision made. The implications were enormous, but my heart told me I was right.

I paid for the necklace, a breathtaking sum, and hurried back to the Mercantile. I longed for the safety of the shop and a return to my own time.

The weight of the necklace felt heavier with each step. Despite Peter's assurance that I could buy the necklace, I felt like I was breaking one of the cardinal rules of time travel. I was supposed to be a guardian of history, not a thief of time. Yet, here I was, with a piece of the past burning a hole through the fabric of time itself.

I couldn't stop wondering what I had done.

CHAPTER 33

Back to Home Base

I MADE MY WAY back to the Mercantile, the Sunset Ruby safely in my hands. It's new box, or its old box? I wasn't sure what to call it.

The familiar tinkle of the shop bell announced my arrival, drawing Peter's attention away from a case of oatmeal he was unpacking.

"Ah, you're back. Let's see if you found what you were looking for." His voice was rich with anticipation.

I approached the counter, gently setting the new old box down and opening it to reveal the necklace inside.

In any other time or place, the presence of two versions of the same artifact could be risky. Within the walls of the old Mercantile—and the future Enchanted Antique Shop—we didn't need to worry about accidental collisions. Just as the portal in the storeroom was a conduit for temporal energies, the brick walls of the shop functioned as a natural insulator. In other words, they were a barrier that protected us from temporal disturbances.

169

The effect was twofold: the walls preserved the integrity of the timeline inside the shop, and they prevented anomalies from seeping into the outside world. As a result, the shop was a sanctuary, where time travelers could interact with artifacts from various eras without fear of creating paradoxes or causing unwarranted ripple effects in the fabric of time.

I opened the hinged lid of the box, where the necklace gleamed against the satin lining. The gemstones caught the light, casting small rainbows around the storeroom. It was hard to believe such a beautiful object could be the center of so much chaos.

Peter gasped, eyes widening. "Marley! It's the Sunset Ruby! You were after the Sunset Ruby?" His surprise echoed around the quiet of the shop.

I nodded, puzzled by his reaction. "I didn't know it had a name. Back at the murder mystery dinner, everyone was calling it the Crimson Teardrop."

Peter shook his head in disbelief. "I remember when Theodore Stevens brought this ruby to Enchanted Springs. It was the talk of the town—at least in the paranormal community."

Peter leaned forward, his voice dropping to a conspiratorial whisper as he began to share the story. "It was said to be discovered in the early 1900s, unearthed from the sands of the Valley of the Queens in Egypt. Legend has it that the ruby was originally set into the diadem of a powerful queen, an enchantress who used the power of song to work magic in her realm."

He paused to make sure I was following. I was familiar with Theodore Stevens, because I'd met his ghost during an investigation at his mansion.

Peter leaned in closer. "They say the Sunset Ruby possesses the power to protect its owner from harm—but at a cost. It's also said to intensify passions, for better or worse. Stevens was a man marked by tragedy and triumph in equal measure, and some say it was the ruby that fueled both."

He straightened up, his voice returning to its usual timbre. "Since Mr. Stevens passed away, we thought the ruby was lost. Imagine. It was only a block away! Did Mr. LaLuna say how he acquired it?"

I nodded. "Yes. Mrs. Stevens' maid gave it to him."

Peter exhaled sharply. "So the rumors were true."

I leaned forward, studying the necklace. "I had no idea it was something so significant. When I found it in the shop, it seemed like any other piece of costume jewelry. Why couldn't I sense anything special about it?"

Peter nodded knowingly. "Eleanor must have shielded its magic. She probably worried about its powerful allure. Can't you feel it? It's not simply a stunning piece of jewelry. It's also steeped in deep, powerful magic."

His eyes narrowed slightly. "Now, Marley, it's time you truly understand what you're dealing with," his tone more serious than before. "You need to open your third eye to see the power in this necklace, above and beyond its physical beauty. It's part of your growth as a witch."

I hesitated, unsure. "How do I do that?"

Peter smiled. "It's not so different from what you do with your other senses, my dear. You simply need to tune in. Close your eyes and reach out toward the energy of the stone. Let it show you its power."

I took a deep breath, took the necklace in my hands, and closed my eyes.

At first, there was nothing. Then, a warm buzz began to flow, moving from my fingertips, across my hands and up my arms. It warmed my heart, both literally and figuratively, as if I was reuniting with an old friend.

"That's it," Peter encouraged, his voice a distant anchor in the swirling sensations. "It's working. I can see the stone glowing."

I kept my eyes closed. The sounds of the mercantile seemed to fade.

Suddenly, I realized I wasn't in Florida anymore. I was standing in a lavish chamber deep within the heart of an Egyptian palace. The walls were adorned with hieroglyphs that danced in the flicker of torchlight, telling stories of gods and mortals. The air carried the dry, warm scent of sandalwood and myrrh, and the subtle fragrance of lotus flowers floating in shallow basins. The chamber echoed with the distant sounds of palace life: the murmur of voices, the clatter of artisans at work, and the rhythmic, melodic chants of priests conducting distant rituals.

In front of me stood a queen, regal and imposing. She wore a magnificent headdress, the ruby set prominently at its center, casting a warm, red glow that bathed her face in a sunset hue.

The vision faded as quickly as it had appeared. I opened my eyes to find myself back in the mercantile, the echo of ancient voices lingering in my ears.

Peter was watching me, smiling softly. "Welcome back," he said.

I told him what I had seen. He nodded, pleased. "Good. It's clearly a powerful relic, but I get the sense that it belongs with you."

I nodded. "When I held it, I didn't feel any sense of danger whatsoever."

"Because you're a good witch, Marley." He smiled. "Seriously, though, it's not a trinket to be trifled with. In the wrong hands, its power could be channeled into something dark and dangerous."

I absorbed this new information, my mind racing. "Which is why Eleanor hid it away."

He nodded. "Exactly. But now that you've connected with it, you should be able to sense when its magic is active. You could even learn to control it."

I sighed. "I have so much to learn."

Peter smiled, his expression softening. "All in due time, my dear. For now, you've made remarkable progress, both in locating the necklace and discerning its true powers."

I nodded, the weight of responsibility settling on my shoulders. I had managed to retrieve a significant piece of our past, but my task was far from over. I still had a murder mystery waiting for me back in my own time.

Peter and I said our goodbyes. I clasped the Sunset Ruby around my neck, along with Calypso's ruby solitaire, and stepped back through the portal in the storeroom. In the blink of an eye, the antique shop welcomed me back to my own time.

I couldn't shake the sense of foreboding that clung to me like a shroud. Had I altered the course of history for better or worse? Or had I merely fulfilled my role in a story that was already written?

CHAPTER 34

Back to the Future

THE PORTAL'S HUM FADED behind me as I stepped out of the storage room. When I passed our display of vintage clothing, I happened to catch a glimpse of the full-length mirror on the wall.

I froze. The reflection staring back at me wasn't my own.

Instead, a young woman from another era gazed out at me. She was unmistakably from the early 1920s, dressed in a strapless satin sheath. The Sunset Ruby lay against her collarbone, gleaming under the flickering light of a lamp that no longer existed in my time.

My hands sought the stone around my neck. As I tentatively touched the string of pearls and the cold, sparkling ruby, the woman in the mirror parallelled my movements precisely. Her fingers traced the same path over the gemstone, which glinted with a strange, inner light. We were more than mirror images. We were linked across time and space by the Sunset Ruby.

I blinked, and my counterpart was gone. My own reflection stared back at me, eyes wide. I reached out, half-expecting my fingers to pass through the mirror, but the cold glass met my touch, solid and real.

There was no time to wonder what it might mean.

I raced back to the Lydia Hotel, my heart pounding with the urgency of everything I had learned. To everyone at the banquet, it would seem as though I'd been gone for a few breathless moments—the few minutes it had taken me to drive back to the shop, and the time it took to return. While I had spent an hour or two in the past, that time away was irrelevant here in the present.

When I skittered back into the ballroom, everything was exactly as I'd seen it last.

The waiter still hovered in mid-step, his tray of champagne flutes balanced in suspended animation. The woman adjusting her dress still tugged at the fabric, captured in motion yet utterly still. The napkin that had begun its floated a few inches above the floor, a ghostly artifact defying gravity. The faces of the partygoers, locked in smiles and mid-conversation, looked vibrant and full of life, but they were eerily silent and immobile.

I had traveled across a century, but here, time had not dared to move a second.

I ducked back into the circle, where my cohorts were still holding hands. Eleanor, Sadie, and Benedict continued to chant, while Gram asked if I was okay.

"I'm fine," I said, whispering as if the rest of the room could hear me. "I had to go back to 1925, but I found the necklace—and its story."

Gram's face softened with relief, a small smile curving her lips. "I see that. Don't take it off. It's bound to you now, and that's a connection we might need before the night is through."

As if in response, the ruby seemed to pulse against my throat. I nodded. "It's a powerful piece."

She smiled. "It's time we let go of the spell. We've been stretching every second to maintain this stasis, but now that you're back we can release the flow of time."

I took a deep breath. Gram offered one final word of caution. "As we lift the spell, stay alert. We'll let Jack continue his investigation, but things may escalate quickly."

CHAPTER 35

A Tick of the Clock

S ADIE CAUGHT MY EYE and nodded slightly, signaling their readiness. The trio recited the final words of their chant, then unclasped their hands.

The air around us seemed to sigh, relaxing as the spell unwound.

As we watched, the frozen scene in the ballroom gradually came back to life. Sounds returned first: the low hum of conversation, the clink of glassware, the distant notes of orchestral music that had been suspended in mid-air. Then movement: guests blinked, shifted in their seats, and continued their activities, unaware of the brief pause in their reality.

Jack, who had been talking to Eddie when time froze, blinked and looked around the room. I wondered if he had sensed a subtle shift in the room's atmosphere. When he spotted me, his eyes narrowed slightly. I tried to act innocent, wiggling my fingers in a playful wave.

"—as I was saying," he continued seamlessly, his voice smooth and unperturbed, "I'll need to talk to all of the performers tonight."

He signaled Lucas, who nodded and stepped onto the stage. Now back in his role as the evening's emcee, he cleared his throat and tapped his glass for attention.

He was enjoying himself. His eyes sparkled with jubilation as he addressed the guests.

"Ladies and gentlemen, what an unexpected and delightfully thrilling turn of events we have experienced tonight!" His voice carried effortlessly across the room. "Our little game of make-believe has taken on a life of its own—or should I say, a death of its own." He winked, enjoying his own joke along with the crowd. Then he continued. "What started as a scripted performance has become a real-life whodunit!"

The guests murmured with excitement, and their faces lit up with intrigue and delight. They seemed to relish the added layer of mystery to their evening, as if Frankie's murder had become the best part of the performance.

He paused for dramatic effect. Everyone's eyes followed Lucius with rapt attention.

"Now we find ourselves not merely spectators, but active participants in an authentic murder mystery! In a few moments, our investigation will proceed, under the professional guidance of Detective Jack Edgewood. I encourage you all to embrace this opportunity, with the same gusto and zeal you brought to this evening's initial performance."

He didn't have to ask twice. The crowd was more enthusiastic than ever. Some people whistled and whooped as if they were at a concert.

"Now, I know you're all as eager as I am to see how this mystery unfolds, but let's not forget the true spirit of our gathering. We're here to enjoy an enchanted evening filled with good food, good company, and a touch of the unexpected!"

Lucius gestured grandly to Clara and Eleanor, who were still standing with our little group. "And what better way to continue our evening than with 'just desserts.'" He winked at his own wordplay. "We won't let good food and good company go to waste!"

Clara and Eleanor exchanged a glance before nodding and heading back into the kitchen.

Lucius clapped his hands together, his energy infectious. "There we go! Now, everyone, take your seats so we can pick up where we left off. Prepare to enjoy the delectable desserts prepared by our marvelous pastry chefs—and keep your eyes and ears open. Who knows what clues might come to light as we feast?"

Jack had resumed his place at my side. I shook my head in confusion. "How can anyone eat with a dead body in the middle of the room?"

His eyes met mine. "Marley, in a room full of immortals, shifters, and fey, the rules of etiquette and decorum don't follow human conventions. Most of us don't fear death the way regular people do."

As if to prove his point, I noticed that the crowd seemed even more animated. Conversations picked up with renewed energy and verve.

I paused to take it all in. "I guess that makes sense. But the people here tonight don't endorse murder, do they?"

"Of course not. Murder is a violation of human law, natural law, free will, and the paranormal moral code."

Fair enough. That still didn't mean I could eat with a dead body at my feet.

Jack gave a small nod, acknowledging my discomfort. "It's unsettling, I know." He glanced around the room, his gaze sharp and assessing. "But even in extraordinary circumstances, we maintain a semblance of normalcy. That's the essence of resilience among the paranormal."

As if on cue, Eddie Hawkner, the head of security, approached. With a quiet incantation, he waved his hand, and a soft, glowing light enveloped the corpse before it disappeared.

I was shocked. "Where did it go? Did he just destroy the evidence?"

Jack answered calmly. "Far from it. If Eddie hadn't transported Frankie's body to a stable location, every bit of evidence would disappear completely at dawn. This way, we ensure everything remains intact, even if we're unable to conclude our investigation tonight."

He looked at me and nodded to reaffirm his words. "Time waits for no one, Marley... except maybe for you."

CHAPTER 36

Setting the Scene

A T THAT MOMENT, LUCIUS stopped by our table. "Jack, if you'll come with me, we'll prepare for the next stage of your investigation."

As they walked away, a procession of waitstaff swept into the ballroom in perfect synchronization. Having burned a ton of calories over the last hundred years, I eagerly took my seat and did what any starving time-traveler would do—I chose all three dessert options.

First came chocolate ganache tarts, so glossy they reflected the light of the chandeliers. Each serving was dotted with edible gold leaf—not just a dusting, but an actual chocolate leaf, dusted with real gold.

Next was sour orange pie, one of my grandmother's specialties. She'd even won a prize for her recipe at the last Founders Festival. The tangy orange filling nestled perfectly in a flaky crust, topped with meringue that danced in perfect peaks.

Then a waiter handed out Espresso Martinis. The blend of espresso and liqueur, garnished with coffee beans, was just the pick-me-up I needed.

At our table, Benedict had plowed his way through two slices of pie, but his attention remained fixated on my necklace.

"It's remarkable," he said, accepting a cup of plain black coffee from a passing server. "That ruby seems to grow brighter and more beautiful with every passing moment. What did you learn about its origin?"

I leaned forward, lowering my voice to ensure privacy. "Well, it's definitely not costume jewelry." I laughed, then glanced around to ensure our conversation stayed between us. "It's actually called the Sunset Ruby, and it's tied to the ancient tombs of Egypt's Valley of the Queens."

Benedict's eyes gleamed with interest. "Remarkable! I believe I've come across stories of the Sunset Ruby in my research. Legend has it that it was worn by queens and high priestesses, It's reported to be one of the most powerful gemstones in existence."

Sadie, who was taking small, delicate bites of chocolate ganache, chimed in with a note of caution. "You know what they say, Marley. With great power comes great responsibility."

Benedict nodded slowly, his expression thoughtful. "Indeed," he agreed. "The potential to use such a gem for good—or ill—is substantial."

I briefly explained my encounter with the necklace's creator, describing his infatuation with the singer and the additional energy intertwined with the piece. "This is the historic version of the necklace. But the version from our timeline, the one Calypso wore tonight, is still missing."

A flicker of frustration passed over Benedict's features. He shook his head, as if he was trying to make sense of it all. "Fascinating, indeed. The complexities of time travel never cease to amaze."

The ballroom fell silent as a gong sounded near the stage and the heavy velvet curtains parted. Gasps of admiration echoed through the room as the set was revealed.

Only a short while ago, this had been the scene of the tragically failed auction. Now, it had been transformed into an elegant dining room. A massive banquet table, long enough to seat a dozen comfortably, stood center stage, heaped with meat, cheese, bread, and fruit. Sparkling decanters of fine wine lined a sideboard, and a warm glow from a marble fireplace bathed dark wood paneling and burgundy wallpaper in a soft light.

Jack stood center stage, commanding attention as he called upon the cast to join him. As the actors took their seats around the table, the atmosphere crackled with anticipation.

Jack looked every bit the leading man as he addressed the performers. "Ladies and gentlemen, thank you for joining me. We're here to discuss the events of this evening. I appreciate your cooperation."

He paused, allowing his words to sink in. "I'll ask each of you to recount your actions leading up to the discovery of Frankie's body. Please be as detailed as possible. And remember, while this may feel like part of the evening's performance, it is a genuine investigation."

With the audience hanging on his every word, Jack began the inquiry, as if he were hosting a reality show. "Let's go over the script. I want to know everyone's parts, especially where you were and what you were supposed to be doing at the time the lights went out."

One by one, the actors and staff began to recount their roles, detailing the scripted interactions and where they were allowed to improvise.

Lucius spoke first, swirling his glass of red wine. "As the emcee, my role was to oversee the auction and engage with the guests," he explained, his voice smooth. "My improvisations were limited to reacting to the bids and keeping the energy high."

Calypso nervously sipped water from a crystal goblet. "I was the focal point, obviously. Before I became known as a singer, I modeled occasionally. Some artists even called me their muse."

Jack's eyes softened slightly. "Calypso, did you see anyone suspicious before the lights went out?"

She shook her head slowly. "No, it all happened so fast. One moment I was posing, and the next, the lights were out, and someone ripped the necklace off my neck." Her blue eyes filled with tears. "I don't know why. It was merely a prop."

Serena, her dark lips curving into a sly smile, sipped from a glass of red wine. "You might say I was playing myself, making my character appear both seductive and dangerous. I was there to stir envy and intrigue, to make the bidding war more intense."

Glen reached for a bread roll and tore off a piece. "I was there for comic effect. I was supposed to make a dramatic play for the necklace, more to impress Cora than anything else."

Cora reached out to take his hand. "I was only pretending to want the necklace. I mostly wanted to know how much Glen would pay to give it to me."

Jasmine twirled a strand of her hair. "I was to flaunt my desire for the necklace. My character's obsession was supposed to add a layer of suspense. And if the play had gone according to plan, Alex and I were to spirit the necklace away together."

Alex poured himself a glass of champagne. "My job was to keep the bids rolling in and to subtly encourage competition among the guests. I was supposed to drop hints about the necklace's history, to add to its mystery and allure."

As the rest of the actors described their roles, my attention drifted to Tommy Tucker, who was playing the part of a security guard. He was outfitted in a faded uniform from another era, the dusty, moth-eaten wool straining slightly across his stomach.

His build was sturdy, verging on stocky, his skin a landscape of pockmarks and scars. His eyes held a certain dullness, as if he had seen too much and cared too little. He seemed more interested in the food than the conversation.

With an oversized fist, he held his hand in an overhand grip, shoveling slices of ham and roast beef into his mouth. Every now and then, he'd gesture, impatiently, for the others to pass him more food.

Jack turned to him next. "And you, Tommy. What did you observe tonight?"

Tommy burped loudly and wiped his mouth with the back of his hand. "Yeah, I can't really tell you nothin'. I was supposed to hang out in the background, looking like I wasn't paying much attention."

Jack fixed him with a penetrating gaze. "Did you see anyone or anything that might have indicated a real theft was about to happen?"

Tommy shook his head. "Nah. My role wasn't really supposed to start until after the murder."

Jack nodded solemnly.

"We know things didn't go as scripted. From everything you've all been saying, the real theft and Frankie's death weren't part of the plan. This tells me someone used the cover of your performance to commit a real crime."

The performers, once a cohesive troupe, now eyed each other warily. Their camaraderie had suddenly evaporated, replaced by tension that pressed down with the weight of suspicion.

CHAPTER 37

Unscripted Revelations

J ACK CONTINUED, HIS GAZE sweeping across the anxious faces. "So everyone had a role to play, and you all had a script to follow. But somewhere along the line, someone deviated from that script."

I noticed a few of them nodding.

"Let's talk motives—real motivations, not the rationales that were scripted for you. Why would anyone want Frankie dead?"

Tension and suspicion crackled through the air like electricity. A heavy silence fell over the cast.

Glen Goldman was the first to speak, his voice tinged with sarcasm. "Well, I never liked the lad, but killing him? Over the top, even for me. If you're sniffing around for motives, perhaps you might want to look in Serena's direction. She and Frankie had a past, didn't they? Not all hearts and flowers, from what I've heard."

Serena's voice was sharp, her eyes flashing with a mixture of indignation and hurt. "Don't be absurd, Glen. Yes, we had our differences, but murder? That's rich coming from you, who's always after more gold. Maybe you wanted to kill Frankie and steal the necklace for real, not just play at it?"

Lucious interjected, his tone icy, casting a suspicious glance around the room. "Or perhaps we should consider Jasmine here. We all know how she's been struggling. She could have used a big score to settle her... debts."

Jasmine turned to face Lucius, her expression icy, her posture rigid with defiance. "That's rich, coming from you. You're as deep in the dirt as anyone here. You hooked me on the stuff, remember?"

As accusations flew, not a single pair of eyes looked away. The audience was captivated, drawn into the drama unfolding before them. Theories flew, not only onstage but around the room, each table buzzing with speculation and intrigue. The spectacle was more gripping than any staged performance could hope to be, blurring the lines between scripted entertainment and raw, unscripted reality.

Lucius cleared his throat. "Let's remember, everyone here has secrets. You're no innocent child, Jasmine. You've come here for years, looking for a bit of a thrill to relieve all the boredom of your immortal existence. I merely make a bit of escape possible."

Calypso finally spoke up, her voice a trembling mix of frustration and fear. "None of us wanted this! Lucius, you think you can manipulate everyone with your debts and secrets, but not everyone is a puppet!"

Her outburst resonated through the room, leaving a silence that felt almost tangible. Everyone was fixed on Lucius, awaiting his response, but it was Jack who reclaimed control.

"Ladies and gentlemen," Jack began, standing from his chair with a deliberate slowness. "Let's take a brief intermission. Refresh your drinks, gather your thoughts. We'll continue short-ly. I'm certain we can expect more revelations shortly."

The actors fled the stage, their facade of control stripped away by the raw emotions that the accusations had unearthed. The audience grumbled and shifted in their seats, reluctant to break away from the spectacle.

In the corner, the spectral orchestra reclaimed the room's focus, their music a soothing balm that floated through the air to ease the tension. The lead violinist, a figure of silvery translucence, drew haunting melodies from her instrument, pulling at the heartstrings of every listener. Beside her, a phan-tom saxophonist, his outline blurred as if he was made of smoke, poured his soul into each note. The pianist, behind a grand piano, played with passion, his fingers gliding over the keys with otherworldly grace.

I watched Jack navigate his way back to our table, his face a mask of professional calm, though his eyes betrayed the rapid calculations behind his composed exterior. I could see the tightness in his gaze. He was a man bracing for the storm's return.

Calypso was hot on his heels, her measured elegance barely concealing the fury brewing within her. She stormed through the throng, a tempest dressed in sequins. Her stride was pur-poseful, her eyes fixed on Jack. She was a portrait of fury in motion, filled with defiance, each step echoing her indigna-tion. I could almost feel the heat of her anger as she closed the distance, ready to confront Jack about the public spectacle that had unfolded.

"What sort of game are you playing here, detective?" Her voice, sharp and commanding, cut through the crowd.

Yet, as she neared, her fiery advance faltered, her eyes suddenly drawn to the necklace around my neck. The sight halted her like a wall. Her stride broke and confusion washed over her face.

"The necklace! You found it? But where?"

The Sunset Ruby pulsed subtly against my skin, its vibrations almost imperceptible.

"Actually, yes, I did find it." I quickly made up a plausible explanation. "It was tucked away at the base of that potted palm." I gestured toward a tree in the corner. "In the chaos, someone must have stashed it there, thinking they could retrieve it later."

The murmur of the crowd ebbed and flowed around us like the tide, pulling back as if to gather strength for the next surge of speculation. The soft, soothing strains of the orchestra contrasted starkly with the sharp tensions still tangible in the air.

I gave Jack a quick glance and shrugged. "I was about to tell you."

Jack eyed the plant I pointed to, his expression tinged with skepticism. His eyes flickered back to me, then my necklace. "That's quite the coincidence," he remarked dryly, clearly unconvinced by the simplicity of my explanation.

"Yes," I agreed. "It was a lucky find."

Calypso held a hand to her heart and took a few deep breaths, then turned back to me. "I'm so relieved. I felt terrible that it was your necklace that got caught up in all this drama."

I seized the opportunity to conclude my improvised story. I nodded and unclasped her ruby solitaire from my neck. "All's well that ends well. Here's your necklace." I extended it toward her like an olive branch.

Calypso accepted the necklace with a nod. "Thank you, Marley. This evening certainly hasn't gone as anyone expected."

Jack's scrutinizing gaze left me feeling exposed. In need of a distraction—and perhaps a stiff drink—I excused myself. "I think I'll go see if they have any more of those Clover Clubs."

Sadie stood, too. "I'll join you." In the wink of an eye, Violet was also at my side.

Together, we moved toward the bar, the ethereal music following us, a gentle reminder of the evening's surreal blend of truth and historical fiction.

CHAPTER 38

A Brief Refreshment

TOGETHER, WE NAVIGATED THROUGH the throng of guests toward the portable bar, our steps synchronizing as we approached.

Lucius spotted me and offered a small, knowing smile as he handed a drink to another guest. "Marley, what can I get for you? Something to calm the nerves, perhaps?" His voice was smooth, betraying none of the tension that underpinned the evening.

"Actually, I'm curious. What was everyone implying about some of your other offerings?"

Lucius paused, his movements slowing as he placed the glass down carefully. His eyes met mine, the affable bartender persona giving way to a more guarded, calculating gaze. "I won't lie," he said, his voice dropping to a whisper that barely carried over the bar. "We live in a world where some prohibitions are still in play. But I save the hard stuff for my clientele that can't be killed. I have a reputation to protect."

His words hung in the air between us, a clear warning veiled within the semblance of bartender banter.

"Then I'll have a gin and tonic, please," I said, deciding to step back from any hint of confrontation. I wanted to keep the lines of communication open. He had confirmed my suspicion, and his response showed he was aware of the stakes.

He swiftly prepared drinks for the three of us. As we walked back to our table, I turned to Violet. "Do you remember when we first met?"

She chuckled softly. "I sure do, doll. It was back on Miami Beach, during one of those stunning sunsets while you were busy with your camera."

I shook my head, a smile tugging at the corners of my lips. "No. Think back further."

She pondered for a moment. "It's possible we met when you were a child. Your grandmother was always popping into the antique shop. You probably came with her."

"Nope, not then." I paused, gauging her reaction. Sadie raised her eyebrows, curious as to where we were going with this conversation.

I looked at both of them and smiled. "Violet, I actually met you for the first time in 1925, back when I went to retrieve this necklace."

"So that's where you were! I knew you disappeared for a minute or two. I could sense a missing tick of the clock, but you know how it is when witches get together. Where did you go?"

"I left to track down this necklace." I gently touched the ruby at my throat. "I traveled back to 1925, and when I got there, I ran into you on the sidewalk."

Her eyebrows shot up in disbelief. "Aw, you're pulling my leg."

"Nope. I remember it like it was yesterday—because it *was* like yesterday for me. I left the Mercantile to go to the Emporium, and there you were, strutting down the sidewalk like you owned it. I thought for a second you had followed me through the portal."

Violet's expression softened into a playful smile. "Nope. I've been here all night." Her smile faltered as a realization dawned. "She set her glass down, her smile broadening. "That explains it! When I saw you that day on the beach in Miami, you seemed so familiar! It was like recognizing someone from a dream."

I took a sip of my gin and tonic. I was enjoying the cosmic lift it gave me, especially since I knew the second drink wouldn't leave me hungover.

"Yep. We only talked for a minute or two. You teased me about being overdressed, but then you had to rush off. You said your husband was waiting in the car." The memory was vivid, almost tangible. "I tried to see where you were going, but you moved too fast. I wish I could have seen him."

Violet's smile slowly faded, replaced by a solemn look as her eyes locked onto mine with an intensity that quieted the surrounding noise. "Wait a minute. Did you say 1925?" Her voice was low.

I nodded, confused by her sudden change in demeanor. "Yes, June 17. Why? Is something wrong?"

For a moment, Violet seemed lost in thought, far away in a sea of memories. Then she focused back on me, her gaze intense, her voice low. "That's too strange to be a coincidence." Her usual light tone was replaced by an unusual somberness. "The day you saw me, when I said my husband was waiting... that was a very significant day for me."

Intrigued and concerned, I leaned closer. "Significant how?" I was trying to tread carefully around what seemed like delicate memories.

Violet took a deep breath, her fingers absently tracing the rim of her glass. "Let's just say, it was a day of changes, of endings and beginnings. I can't go into it now, not here," she glanced around the bustling room, her voice dropping to a hush. "But someday, I'll tell you the whole story. For now, to realize that you and I first met on that particular day... it's more important than you realize."

She leaned forward to kiss me briefly on the cheek, then excused herself. "The stars are beautiful tonight. I'm just going to step out on the terrace to watch them for a moment."

As Violet slipped outside, I caught sight of Jasmine lingering near the fringes of the ballroom. Her expression was somber and contemplative. I told Sadie I would meet her back at the table, and then I approached Jasmine, my curiosity piqued by the unresolved threads of her story.

"Jasmine," I started, keeping my voice low. "Earlier tonight, I overheard your conversation with Alex. It wasn't just about the play, was it? The two of you had something else planned."

Jasmine's gaze met mine, a flicker of surprise crossing her features before she masked it with a resigned smile. "Yes, Marley. You're right. We weren't talking about the play."

I leaned in, intrigued. "What were you talking about?"

She sighed, her eyes searching mine for a hint of understanding. "I've lived long enough to admit when I need help," she confessed. Her voice was low and quiet. "I'd finally agreed to let Alex take me to treatment, and we were planning to leave after the performance. My... addiction, it's not something I can fight alone anymore."

The revelation added layers to Jasmine's character I hadn't anticipated. Here was a woman, seemingly invincible, laid bare by her vulnerabilities. "And the necklace? The theft, and the murder?"

Jasmine shook her head, a faint smile tugging at her lips. "We had nothing to do with that. We were simply planning to make a quiet exit, but things got out of hand before we could follow through."

I nodded. "I'm glad you're seeking help, Jasmine. I think you're really brave, and I think you've got what it takes to recover."

She looked away for a moment, collecting herself before she met my gaze again. "It's funny, isn't it? No matter how long we live, or how much we learn, we still have our demons."

CHAPTER 39

Back to Business

THE INTERMISSION ENDED ABRUPTLY when Eddie, the head of security, stepped forward with an announcement. "Ladies and gentlemen, it's time we bring this performance to a close and resolve the matters at hand." His eyes swept the crowd before he turned to Jack. "Detective, we need to wrap this up. It's clear who the culprit is."

Jack, who had been sipping a glass of water, looked up. His expression was one of wary curiosity. "And who do you think that is, Eddie?" he asked. His tone was neutral, yet probing.

Eddie's eyes narrowed slightly, and he nodded toward one of the actors who had played a particularly shady character in the staged mystery. "Clearly, it's Glen Goldman. He as much as confessed on stage, didn't he? His motives were plain for everyone to see. He killed Frankie to steal the necklace, which, as we all know, is worth a considerable sum."

Murmurs rippled through the crowd, heads turning to Glen, whose face paled under the scrutiny. He looked confused and alarmed, and he shook his head vehemently.

"I didn't kill anyone, and I didn't steal the necklace. I only came here to play a bit part in an amateur production and get a free meal."

I scanned the room, noting the slight shifts in demeanor. Everyone seemed a touch more guarded, perhaps a result of the whispered secrets and shared suspicions that had flavored our break.

Jack seemed unfazed by Eddie's confident accusation. He stood up from our table.

"If that's the case, Eddie," Jack began, his voice steady and clear, "why is the necklace still here?" He pointed toward me, drawing the eyes of everyone in the room to the glittering piece still securely around my neck.

Eddie's face tightened, his eyes darting momentarily toward the necklace before returning to Jack with a forced calmness. "Glen made a mistake, obviously. Or maybe your little girlfriend grabbed it while no one was looking. We don't know all the details yet."

Jack crossed his arms, his gaze not leaving Eddie. "Or perhaps the necklace was never stolen in the first place. Maybe what happened to Frankie had nothing to do with theft."

Eddie's posture stiffened, and he took a step back, his composure beginning to crack. "You can speculate all you want later, but we still need to resolve this tonight."

Jack nodded. "We will resolve it." His tone was resolute. "But we will do it thoroughly. We won't settle for convenient answers. We'll uncover the whole truth."

Jack held up his hand to quiet Eddie's protests, then turned to me.

"Marley, there's more to that necklace than meets the eye, isn't there? It's not merely an accessory. It's at the center of everything that's happened."

I nodded. "It is, and it isn't. And after seeing the mystery unfold, I think we've been witnessing two separate crimes."

Before I could explain, Benedict spoke up.

"Marley, if that necklace is indeed as significant as it seems—worth killing for, even—I suggest you let me keep it safe. The risk of holding onto it might be greater than you realize."

I hesitated, feeling the Sunset Ruby thrumming against my neck. "I appreciate your concern, Benedict, but it's not just a piece of jewelry. It's a clue, and it's safest with me until we solve this mystery."

As the murmurs in the room grew louder, Benedict stood and stepped toward me.

"Marley," he said, his voice low but insistent, cutting through the noise of the gathering. "Give me the necklace. It's for your own safety."

He held out his hand, expecting me to hand it to him. The room's attention shifted to me, awaiting my response. Jack watched silently, his expression unreadable but his eyes sharp.

I shook my head no. "Benedict, I appreciate your concern." My voice was steady despite the churn of anxiety beneath my calm exterior. "But this necklace seems to be at the heart of everything tonight. If I give it up now, who's to say what will happen to it? Who's to say it won't disappear again?"

Benedict's brow furrowed, and he glanced briefly at Jack before responding. "I assure you, I only wish to protect you. You've become a target by wearing it. Let me safeguard it with my magic until this case is resolved."

From across the room, Calypso called out with a seemingly innocent question. "It is just a prop, right? Marley, didn't you say your necklace was costume jewelry?"

Her tone was casual, but her eyes were locked onto mine, challenging me. I hesitated, the weight of the truth heavy on my tongue.

CHAPTER 40

Give Me the Necklace

BEFORE I COULD FORMULATE a response, Benedict erupted, his voice tinged with frustration and urgency. "Clearly, it's a magical artifact. Anyone with half a magical bone in their body can tell that necklace is enchanted. Costume jewelry? Hardly!"

His declaration caused a ripple of reactions among the crowd. Some looked intrigued, others skeptical. The room buzzed with renewed speculation.

Jack raised an eyebrow, turning his attention to Benedict. "Is that so? And how can you be sure of that, Professor?"

Benedict met Jack's gaze squarely, his posture stiffening. "I've been around magic long enough to recognize its signature. That necklace doesn't just hold historical value; it possesses energies that can be sensed, and manipulated."

I felt all eyes on me again, the air thick with curiosity and doubt. Swallowing hard, I finally spoke up, my voice small but clear. "Benedict is right. It's more than a simple prop."

Jack nodded slowly, processing the information. "That complicates things."

Benedict, sensing the growing intrigue and concern, added, "Which is all the more reason to ensure its safety. Marley, you must understand the risk you've casually strung around your neck."

The room had fallen into an uneasy silence after my admission of the necklace's magical properties. Benedict, seizing the moment, stepped forward with a look of profound certainty on his face.

"That necklace," he declared, his voice carrying across the room, "is the long-lost Sunset Ruby. I recognized it the moment I laid eyes on it."

His words landed like a stone in a still pond, sending ripples of shock and murmurs through the gathered crowd.

Jack's eyes narrowed slightly, skepticism and interest flickering across his face. "The Sunset Ruby, you say? That's a bold claim. What makes you so sure?"

Benedict didn't bother to tell him that I had already confided the stone's origin. His gaze didn't waver as he addressed Jack and the room. "The color, the cut, the unmistakable magical aura it emits—it matches every description from the texts and tales I've studied over the years. Marley herself has confirmed it. There's no doubt in my mind about its identity."

Jack stepped closer, positioning himself between Benedict and me. "If this is indeed the Sunset Ruby, then the case takes on even greater significance. We're not dealing with a simple crime of opportunity."

Benedict nodded in agreement, his earlier insistence gaining a new layer of urgency. "Exactly. Whoever killed Frankie must have known what he was after. This isn't about money—it's about power. The kind of power that can change the world."

Benedict's voice grew fervent as he continued, his eyes alight with a zeal that hinted at obsession.

"That necklace is the whole reason I came to Enchanted Springs. My research, years of it, led me inevitably to the conclusion that the Sunset Ruby had been hidden here, in this shabby backwater town. I came to claim it for the Custodians of the Veil, so we can use this magical artifact to its fullest potential!"

As he spoke, his demeanor shifted from scholarly to fanatic, his hands gesturing wildly, his voice rising with each word. The room's atmosphere tensed, and guests exchanged uneasy glances as they absorbed the implications of his declaration.

Sadie rose to stand beside him. Her expression had transformed from mild curiosity to wild alarm. She placed a gentle hand on his arm in an attempt to calm him. "Benedict, you need to take a moment. Let's not get ahead of ourselves."

But Benedict shook her off. His focus locked on the necklace around my neck. "No, I will not back down! Sadie, you don't understand! The power within this gem—it's not just a bauble to be admired! It has capabilities that could benefit the world—or doom us all completely if it falls into the wrong hands. We can't let it linger here, hidden away from those who know how to use it responsibly!"

I found my voice. "Benedict," I said. "I appreciate your passion, but you're scaring people. We need to discuss this calmly, without making rash decisions based on unchecked emotions."

Sadie nodded in agreement, her worried eyes meeting mine. "Marley is right, Benedict. We need to think this through. Let's sit down and talk about it rationally."

Just then, Calypso stood up, her voice cutting through the cacophony with startling clarity.

"You can all stop fighting amongst yourselves. I don't know what she's wearing, but it's an imitation."

Her eyes flashed with defiance. "I have the true Sunset Ruby."

CHAPTER 41

One Ruby to Rule them All

T HE ROOM FELL INTO a stunned silence, all eyes turning toward Calypso.

She reached into the bodice of her sequined gown, withdrawing a necklace that pulsated with a deep, inner light. The gem at its center glowed ominously, its crimson hue stark against the dim lighting of the room.

Benedict, momentarily taken aback, quickly regained his composure and scoffed. "That's impossible! You're bluffing. There can't be two Sunset Rubies."

Calypso laughed, a sound that chilled the air with its intensity. "Oh, but there is only one, Benedict. And it seems you've been chasing a decoy. While you've been distracted with that cheap imitation trinket, I've had the true Sunset Ruby all along."

As she raised the gem, a subtle hum filled the room, the air vibrating with unseen energy.

She waved it triumphantly in the air and snarled, daring anyone to stop her. "It's mine! It was created in my honor, imbued with my gifts, my talents. It has the power to bring my voice—and my visions—to life. I accidentally let it slip through my hands all those years ago, but now that I've regained possession, I intend to make sure I never lose sight of it again."

Jack stepped between Calypso and the rest of the room. "Enough, Calypso! If what you say is true, you're endangering us all. You need to step back and let us handle this responsibly."

Calypso's eyes narrowed. "Handle this? You think you can contain such power? I was chosen by destiny to wear the Sunset Ruby, once and forever!"

Sadie moved closer to me, her expression one of concern. "Marley, we need to do something. If she has the Sunset Ruby from the past, and it's as powerful as she claims, this could get dangerous."

With a triumphant smirk, Calypso clasped the necklace around her neck. No sooner had the gem touched her skin than the air around her began to crackle with energy.

Calypso cackled as the air around her shimmered and twisted. "Behold the power of the Sunset Ruby!" she cried, her voice echoing across the room.

The chandeliers swayed as if caught in a tempest, and the ground beneath our feet vibrated with the force of an earthquake.

Calypso began to sing, a dramatic, coursing version of the song that had been haunting me for days. With each line, her voice grew louder, and louder, until she was screaming.

> *The ruby sun sets,*
> *the day fades away.*
> *I have no regrets,*
> *FOR I AM HERE TO STAY!*

Jack shouted over the tumult, trying to regain control of the situation. "Everyone, get back! This is dangerous!"

He moved to pull Calypso away from the center of the storm she had unleashed, but an invisible force field repelled him, knocking him back.

Benedict, his face pale with fear and realization, yelled to me over the roar of the storm. "Marley! She's created a paradox! The same object can't exist simultaneously in two places—it's tearing the fabric of reality!"

The air grew heavier, the pressure mounting as if time and space were being squeezed around us. Both rubies—the one Calypso wore, and the one around my neck—were glowing brightly, pulsating with a rhythm that felt alive and sentient.

Calypso, now clearly struggling to maintain control, was no longer the confident sorceress; she was a conduit for a power that threatened to consume her.

As the storm intensified, Benedict lunged toward Calypso. He, too, was thrown back.

Sadie grabbed my arm, pulling me toward what she hoped would be safety. "We have to do something, Marley! If she doesn't release the ruby, it could unravel time itself!"

CHAPTER 42

Just Desserts

THE CHANDELIERS SWAYED OMINOUSLY as the storm around Calypso grew in intensity. I felt a surge within me, a commanding pull toward the gale that enveloped her. Almost involuntarily, I found myself walking toward her, my feet moving as if guided by the very currents of time itself.

Time around us seemed to slow to a crawl. Calypso watched me approach, her expression contorting into a grotesque mask of disdain.

"Calypso," I called out, my voice steady despite the chaos. "That necklace was never meant for you. It was crafted with Arabella Delarosa in mind, designed to complement her spirit—not to be wielded as a weapon."

Calypso's eyes, alight with a fierce, cold fire, met mine. Her face twisted with old resentments as she spat back. "Arabella? Hah! She was nothing. A nobody. People were beguiled by her innocence, her eagerness to please."

She laughed, a hollow, bitter laugh. "In a way, you kind of remind me of her. You both have a limited talent, but neither one of you knows how to use it."

She caressed the ruby at her throat and her eyes stopped focusing on me. Once again, she was remembering the past with dark nostalgia. "She was a temporary star in my sky, and I simply expedited her fall."

"You killed her?" The words left my lips before I could consider them.

"Let's just say I hastened her exit, stage left."

At that moment, my resolve crystallized. The tempest around us mirrored Calypso's inner turmoil, and I reached deep within my own spirit, tapping into a raw, untested power. The air shimmered with potential as I recited an incantation more instinctual than learned.

A thunderous crack echoed through the room as a vortex opened in the floor beneath her feet. She hovered briefly above it, her expression morphing from triumph to terror. She opened her mouth to scream, but a roaring, whirling wind drowned out any sound.

Everyone else covered their ears. The building shook. Windows rattled. Bits of plaster fell from the ceiling, crumbling down on people, tables, and chairs. And then, before our horrified eyes, Calypso vanished, consumed by the vortex, sucked down through the floor, tumbling through the void and disappearing into the distant recesses of the earth beneath our feet.

And then, as suddenly as it had begun, it ended. Calypso was gone, swallowed by the earth itself. The vortex closed, the room returned to normal, and only my labored breathing punctuated the stillness.

Silence crashed down upon us like the aftermath of a storm. I stood alone in the epicenter of the vanished chaos, the weight of the evening's events anchoring me to the spot.

Calypso's ambitions, the legend of the Sunset Ruby, and the shadows of the past had all converged. The echoes of Calypso's silent scream seemed to linger in the air, a reminder of the power and peril that had passed.

As the guests looked at each other in shock and awe, resuming slow, cautious movements, Jack approached me. He took both of my hands in his.

"Marley, I don't think I've ever seen cosmic justice meted out so quickly, or so spectacularly."

I managed a small, weary smile, feeling the adrenaline begin to ebb from my veins. "Sometimes, the universe aligns." I gazed at the spot where Calypso had vanished.

I touched the ruby at my neck, both to calm my nerves and reassure myself that it was still there.

I coughed as a puff of black smoke shot out from the center of the stone. Was that the haze I had noticed obscuring Calypso's face earlier? The dark cloud swirled up toward the ceiling, its tendrils thick with the tang of ancient grief and modern guilt.

But as the cloud of negativity evaporated, the gemstone felt lighter, brighter, and warmer to the touch. Prisms of soft pink light emanated from the ruby. They cascaded around the room, painting the walls and ceiling with dancing colors.

People in the crowd sighed as they witnessed the spectacle. The air itself seemed to thrum with a gentle power, enveloping everyone in a tender hush of wonder, as they watched the transformation unfold, spellbound by the beauty and the magic of the moment.

Then, from the heart of the light, the spectral figure of a young woman emerged. I'd seen her before, looking at me from the mirror in the antique shop. Her auburn hair shimmered with hints of gold, and her hazel eyes were luminous.

I stared in wonder. "Arabella?" She looked at me and smiled.

In that moment, I realized that Calypso had been right: we shared a certain innocence. It wasn't naivete, however. It was a deep-seated belief in the enduring power of hope and love, a purity of spirit that could not be tarnished by time or tribulation.

"Yes. And I recognize you too, Marley." Her voice was a soft melody that somehow carried clearly across the room, imbued with a spectral clarity. "Thank you for setting me free."

Arabella's gaze swept across the crowded room, her expression alight with tender recognition. There, at the bar, stood Daniel DeLuna. The jeweler I'd met in 1925 was waiting for her, a patient smile gracing his lips. In one hand, he held two crystal flutes, the champagne inside shimmering with the promise of celebration.

As if they were the only two people in the world, Daniel's eyes locked with Arabella's, and a soft, knowing smile spread across his face. It was the look of a man who had waited a century for this reunion, standing there as though he were simply early for their first date, not decades late.

Arabella moved toward him, her form gaining substance with each step, as if the very act of approaching him wove her back into the fabric of life they should have shared.

When she reached him, she didn't speak at first. Instead, she took a deep breath, and her voice, clear and haunting, filled the ballroom. She sang the same lines that Calypso had sung to open the evening. Now, however, the lyrics now imbued with a depth of meaning and emotion that resonated through every corner of the room.

The ruby sun sets,
The day fades away.
I have no regrets.
My love is here to stay.

Daniel's eyes welled with tears as he listened, the sound of her voice a melody he thought he'd lost forever. He reached out to her, his hands trembling slightly as if he could scarcely believe she was real. As her song tapered into a soft echo, he pulled her close and greeted her with a tender kiss that spoke of long-awaited dreams and promises.

Together, they turned toward us and raised their glasses in recognition of everything that had been lost—and everything that had been found again, their bond sealed by time, but unbroken by its passage.

She reached out, touching the jeweler's cheek with a hand that, though translucent, carried the warmth of life. He clasped her hand, holding it against his heart. "I've never forgotten the sound of your voice, Arabella. I never stopped believing you'd come back to me."

Around them, the atmosphere softened, the lingering tension dissolving into a scene of reunion and redemption. As Arabella and the jeweler faded away to celebrate their reunion in private, a spontaneous round of applause erupted throughout the ballroom. All the world loves a lover, and this particular happy ending was celebrated with genuine enthusiasm.

I waited a moment, then I held up a hand to slow their roll.

"Let's not get ahead of ourselves. There were two separate crimes tonight. We still have a murder to solve."

CHAPTER 43

Eddie's Endgame

J ACK NODDED, SIGNALING ME to continue.

I turned to face Eddie, who stood rigid, his gaze darting nervously.

"Eddie, you've been the head of security here for a long time." My voice was steady, and the crowd was captivated.

He nodded, a hint of pride in his voice. "Longer than you've been alive."

"And Frankie was a regular here that whole time, wasn't he?" I pressed, watching his reaction closely.

"Yes, he was." His eyes narrowed slightly as he tried to gauge where my questions were leading.

Drawing a deep breath, I continued. "And during that time, Frankie never really gave up his old habits, did he? There were thefts and petty crimes, on a regular basis, jeopardizing the speakeasy's reputation and threatening your position here."

Lucius, who had been listening intently, suddenly interjected. His voice filled with disbelief and anger. "Eddie, you told me you had it all under control!"

Eddie's response was defiant, his voice rising slightly with frustration. "I did! I took care of the problem, once and for all, tonight! I shot Frankie dead with a silver bullet, guaranteed to ban him from this plane for good. His ghost is gone, and I'm not sorry."

The room fell silent, the implication of his words hanging heavily in the air.

Jack stepped forward. "Eddie, there's something that doesn't add up. The dueling pistol you showed us. What was that all about?

Eddie shook his head and shrugged. "That was my plan B. If things had gone south, I needed a fall guy. Luckily, you trusted me to handle all the evidence, so I didn't need to frame that idiot waiter."

"But why?" I pressed, struggling to understand his motives. "Why involve someone who had nothing to do with this?"

Eddie shrugged, his expression hardening. "In this business, you always need an exit strategy. It's not personal; it's precaution. If I couldn't clean up the mess myself, I needed someone else to take the fall. It's that simple."

I shook my head, disgusted not only by his actions but by his callous justification. "You were willing to ruin an innocent man's life just to cover your own murderous ways."

He met my gaze, unflinching. "In our line of work, it's about survival, Marley. You do what you must to protect your interests. If you're not willing to make the hard choices, you're not cut out for this job."

The room, once buzzing with casual chatter, was quiet. The gravity of Eddie's confession had left the audience in stunned silence.

Jack nodded toward Tommy, the actor playing a security guard, who had been watching, open mouthed, with the rest of the cast.

"Tommy, it looks like it's time for your big scene."

The wheels spun slowly, but Jack's meaning finally clicked into place. Tommy struggled to his feet, then lumbered to Eddie's side. He managed to unclip the handcuffs from his costume and clamp them around Eddie's wrists. The sound of the metal clicking shut echoed through the room.

The audience, caught up in the drama, burst into a rousing round of applause.

Jack held up a hand to quiet the crowd.

"And Calypso?" Jack asked. "What was that all about?"

I was happy to explain. "That was the second crime. The theft was completely unrelated to Frankie's murder. Calypso ripped the Sunset Ruby from her own neck, because she knew the blackout was coming. It was part of the script—so she improvised her own ending."

Now that the full truth had been revealed, I realized I needed to sit down. I moved toward my chair, and Jack held my hand as I took my seat.

I shook my head. "Honestly, I think I feel sorry for Calypso. In her greed and delusion, she thought she could harness its full power. She never realized the gem wasn't simply a source of power, but a beacon of balance. When she tried to wield it against the natural order, it rejected her."

Jack looked thoughtful, his gaze drifting over the slowly calming crowd. "It's a lot to process. Eddie's actions, Calypso's greed... it's as if tonight peeled back the surface of our world to reveal the depths beneath."

Which reminded me. Benedict had been unusually quiet since his outburst about the Sunset Ruby.

CHAPTER 44

Benedict's Betrayal

I TURNED TOWARD HIM. I wanted to make a few things clear.

"Benedict, your behavior tonight was abhorrent. I can't believe how you treated me."

His eyes met mine, and for a moment, he seemed to struggle with himself. Finally, he sighed, and any fight that was left drained out of him.

"Marley, I apologize. My passion for protecting magical artifacts can get the better of me. I let my zeal cloud my judgment."

I crossed my arms and shook my head, not quite ready to lower my guard. "It wasn't just passion, Benedict. You tried to manipulate me."

He nodded, looking genuinely remorseful. "You're right, and I'm sorry. I've been chasing the Sunset Ruby for so long, I lost sight of why I started in the first place—to protect, not to possess. Seeing it tonight, so close... I got carried away."

As Benedict's apology hung in the air, a new voice cut through the tentative truce.

"I heard everything." Grandma Clara was glaring at Benedict, hands on her hips. Eleanor stood beside her, scowling and shaking her head in disgust.

Gram launched into an old-fashioned dressing down, and Benedict took it all in like a scolded child.

"Benedict, you crossed a lot of lines tonight. Marley might forgive you, but your actions demand further review. Because I'm a member of the local Council of Guardians, I'm obligated to notify the Higher Council of Guardians whenever a trusted teacher or guide abuses his position of authority." She shook her head sadly. "As a professor and well-regarded researcher, you should have known better. I *know* you knew better."

She took a deep breath, then sighed. "But that's enough from me. I've reached out to the Higher Council, and there's someone here who would like a word with you."

I recognized the man who suddenly materialized at my grandmother's side. I didn't know his name; I simply called him the Traveler. He had kept an eye on me early in my training, when I took a few unauthorized trips to the 1940s. He was dressed, now as then, simply but impeccably in a well-tailored dark jacket, a crisp white shirt, and plain black trousers—the epitome of understated power. Because I'd been on the receiving end of a few stern words, I knew that he was firm, but fair.

He stepped forward and asked Benedict to stand.

"Professor Cumberland, your actions have raised concerns that necessitate a review by the Higher Council." His voice was calm but carried an undeniable edge of seriousness. "You will come with me. Your cooperation is expected."

Benedict stiffened, his earlier contrition shifting into a mix of resignation and resolve. "Understood." He nodded slowly, then turned to me. "Marley, I hope my future actions will show my true intent more clearly than my words tonight."

Without another word, he walked toward the Traveler, his posture one of a man ready to face the consequences of his own actions. As they disappeared together in a flash of light, my grandmother addressed the room with a determined nod of her chin.

"All right," she declared. "Now we can celebrate."

CHAPTER 45

Dancing 'Til Dawn

L UCIUS CLAPPED HIS HANDS. and his army of servers came swarming into the ballroom with magnums of champagne.

"To Marley and Jack!" Lucius proclaimed. "Two mysteries solved for the price of one—with hours to go before sunrise!"

The crowd cheered, rising to their feet in a standing ovation. As corks popped and the bubbly began to flow, the orchestra launched into a rousing rendition of "Ain't Misbehavin'." I laughed at the irony.

Jack wrapped me in a warm embrace, but Sadie and Violet pushed him out of the way so they could hug me, too.

Someone shouted from the back. "This was the best murder mystery party *ever*!"

Dancing followed, of course. That orchestra was there for a reason. As Violet had said, the patrons at *Spirits* knew how to cut a rug.

After the chaos had settled down a bit, Sadie and I found a quiet corner to catch our breath. We sat together and she turned to me with a smile.

"You know, I did have something to tell you about that record you asked me to research. I did some digging back at the university. As it turns out, the singer was a young woman named Arabella Delarosa—and she disappeared mysteriously in the early 1920s."

I shook my head sadly. "Well, now we know the rest of the story. What a waste."

Sadie nodded in agreement. "I know. Calypso admitted to stealing Arabella's life, but she stole her voice, too. I'm so glad you helped her reclaim it."

The eerie connection between Arabella's lost voice and the necklace had been an unexpected revelation—but now that Arabella's spirit had been freed, it felt like the ruby's curse had been lifted, too.

As we returned to the dance floor, Jack swept me into his arms. As he led me through several waltzes—and a few Charlestons—I felt glad to be back in my hometown. Enchanted Springs was more than a peculiar place with a paranormal population. It was a city where the past was intertwined with the present, and the future promised unlimited possibilities.

Tonight had been more than a magical mystery, solved in spectacular style. It was also a celebration of community, of coming together to share in the extraordinary. And as the evening wound down, with laughter and tales of adventure filling the air, I knew that this enchanted evening would be remembered as one of the most thrilling events in Enchanted Springs' history.

I couldn't help noticing that Violet was sitting alone at our table. I nudged Jack to dance with Sadie, then I joined my favorite flapper.

Violet gazed wistfully to the empty chair beside her, and she seemed far away from the merriment. She sighed softly, her voice tinged with a longing that cut through the festive atmosphere. "I did hope tonight would be the night he came back for me."

At her words, I followed her eyes to the empty chair. But as I looked back at Violet, I caught a fleeting glimpse of a figure in the doorway—a handsome ghost in a pinstriped suit, with a silk vest and a matching bow tie. He stared at Violet with a look of longing on his face.

"You mean your husband?"

She nodded, her eyes not leaving the empty chair beside her. "Yes, I always hope—"

"Is that him, in the doorway?" The words spilled from me as I pointed.

Just as Violet's head turned to look, he disappeared in a wisp of smoke. "Where?" she asked.

Well, this was awkward.

"You know what? It's late, and I'm tired, and I think I'm seeing things. There's no one there."

Violet turned toward me, and her eyes met mine with a look of silent understanding.

"You've been through a lot tonight, kitten. I take back everything I ever said about you being dull. You might just be the most interesting person I've ever met."

—⚬—

CHAPTER 46

A Magical Feast

THANK YOU FOR VISITING Enchanted Springs, where ghosts are friendly, magic is real, and time is anything but linear!

If you'd like the recipes for all the aperitifs, appetizers, and entrees in this story, keep reading! You'll learn how you can get a copy of *A Magical Feast: Recipes for an Enchanted Evening*.

This full-color recipe collection invites you to recreate the menu that delighted partygoers in *Enchanted Evening*, with photos by Marley Montgomery.

For even more bonus content related to this book—and the rest of the Enchanted Antique Shop series—visit my website at CielleKenner.com.

A Magical Feast

Step into a world where magic is always brewing.

This story might have ended, but you can keep the party going with *A Magical Feast*. This full-color recipe collection invites you to recreate the menu that delighted partygoers in *Enchanted Evening*, with photos by Marley Montgomery.

Discover the sparkling cocktails crafted by Lucius Black, the enigmatic proprietor of *Spirits*—the paranormal speakeasy hidden in plain sight.

Recreate the sumptuous entrées prepared by Sylvia Robinson, Enchanted Springs' best-known chef.

And bring your own enchanted evening to a sweet conclusion with delectable desserts perfected by Clara Montgomery, owner of the Enchanted Oven bakery.

Whether you're hosting a grand gala or an intimate gathering of friends, the dishes in *A Magical Feast* will bring a touch of magic to your table. Prepare to dazzle your guests with flavors that are as enchanting as all the stories from the Enchanted Antique Shop series.

Available online or at your favorite bookstore.

ISBN 979-8325648380

ASIN B0D46NQF8S

Made in the USA
Columbia, SC
22 November 2024

46766952R00130